Copyright © 2023 by Anna Worth

Glitter Bombs & Second Chances by Anna Worth

All rights reserved.

No part of this publication may be reproduced, distributed, or transmitted in any form or by any means, including photocopying, recording, or other electronic or mechanical methods, without the prior written permission of the publisher, except as permitted by U.S. copyright law. For permissions, please contact *annaworthwrites@gmail.com*.

The story, all names, characters, and incidents portrayed in this production are fictitious. No identification with actual persons (living or deceased), places, buildings, and products is intended or should be inferred.

Book Cover by MIBLART

First edition 2023

GLITTER BOMBS & SECOND CHANCES

Anna Worth

To the dreamers and recovering (or not) people pleasers. May the next dream be yours.

Contents

	Tropes & Trigger Warnings	1
1.	Chapter One: Status Quo	3
2.	Chapter Two: Unmoored	10
3.	Chapter Three: In Her Wake	17
4.	Chapter Four: Picking Up the Pieces	24
5.	Chapter Five: Treading Water	32
6.	Chapter Six: The First Test	41
7.	Chapter Seven: The Fallout	50
8.	Chapter Eight: Unto the Breach	63
9.	Chapter Nine: A Fitting Farewell	76
10.	Chapter Ten: Moving Forward	81
11.	Chapter Eleven: That Is My Circus	92
12.	Chapter Twelve: The Picnic	101
13.	Chapter Thirteen: The Storm	112

14.	Chapter Fourteen: Shelter	123
15.	Chapter Fifteen: A Very Important Date	138
16.	Chapter Sixteen: A More Private Picnic	148
17.	Chapter Seventeen: Here Comes the Rain	157
18.	Chapter Eighteen: Lights, Camera, Action	167
19.	Chapter Nineteen: The Aftershocks	174
20.	Chapter Twenty: The Ball	184
21.	Chapter Twenty-One: Final Call	189
22.	Chapter Twenty-Two: Hail Mary, Take Two	209
Author's Note		214
Acknowledgements		216

Tropes & Trigger Warnings

- Second Chance, Small Town Romance

- Open Door Romance

- Panic/Anxiety Attack (described on page)

- Death of Pseudo-Parent

- Grief

- Planned Parental Abduction/Custody Issues (Off Screen – Mentioned, Not Main Characters)

Chapter One: Status Quo

Madison's fingers snapping in front of her face derailed Leah's thoughts from the latest Situation Normal: All Fucked Up.

"Shit, sorry," she said with a sigh. "No more thinking about work, even if Mrs. Johnson is absolutely crazy and driving our client and us insane."

"Good girl," Madison said with a teasing grin. "Have a cookie." She pushed the plate of cheesy breadsticks closer to Leah.

Madison stuck her tongue out when Leah raised an eyebrow. "Any good thing can be a cookie. Don't be pedantic, or I'll hoard the cheesy goodness."

Leah laughed, forcing herself back to the here and now with Madison. The pile of work waiting for her at the office would be there tomorrow. They had left work late together, as usual. On the way out, they'd decided to head to their favorite sober bar, fittingly named The Bar—the absolute best cure for testy clients, opposing parties, and the stress that went with them.

Madison studied her, waiting until she had Leah's attention. "What would you have done, if you hadn't become a lawyer?"

Leah blinked rapidly, processing the abrupt question. "Subject change much?"

Madison stuck out her tongue. "Well, you've already explained why you can't give me relationship advice, and I've explained to you why I can't give you relationship advice."

Leah winced at the reminder. The relationship with fondest memories for her was her college roommate slash fuck buddy. They had fallen into a mutually beneficial arrangement after Leah's college boyfriend slept with said roommate without telling her he was involved, much less that he was involved with Leah. Madison, on the other hand, had a string of relationships with shitty men, the most memorable of whom stole her mattress *because it was the best sleep he had ever gotten.*

"Okay, yes, fair enough. But," Leah added, "you know this conversation won't pass the Bechdel test."

Madison snorted. "Whatever, nerd. I would've gone into private investigations. Your turn."

Leah laughed. "Whoa, now I'm going to need some more information about that. That could've been a nice gig."

"Ah, yes, the living paycheck to paycheck and unreliable income combination sounds swell."

Leah tipped her glass to Madison in silent acknowledgment.

"Hence why I am not a private investigator," Madison said with a wave of her hand. When Leah raised an eyebrow, requiring more information, Madison pushed her lip out into a fake pout. "I brought this on myself, didn't I?"

"You sure did, cupcake."

Madison rolled her eyes before shooting Leah a grin to bely the irritation. "My dad was a PI, and I wanted to follow in his footsteps. He convinced me to try something else, work in a field that could offer more stability. And I get to do a little detective work here and there. Help track down some assets, look through the financials for something fishy, et cetera.

Now," she added, voice firm, "your turn."

Leah's eyes crinkled with her amusement. Madison excelled at keeping a conversation on track... when she wanted it to stay on said track.

"Alright," she said slowly. "I would've moved in with my Aunt Sadie. She lives on some acreage just outside Clearwater, not too far from here. Historic farmhouse, original to the property, indoor arena, and a shop for me to fool around with my art. I still go out there every weekend I can, work on my latest piece. Less chance of setting off my place's demon-possessed smoke detector or suffocating on the fumes that way."

Leah smiled softly. Talking about the little hobby farm she and Sadie loved so dearly was its own balm. Just thinking about the place helped bring her back to baseline. Shaking herself out of her mental happy place, she shot Madison a quick grin.

"The local schools have at least one tour of the farmhouse every year as a field trip. I lived with Sadie my last year of high school after my parents moved away, so I wouldn't have to be the new girl senior year.

"We talked a lot about doing something together with her space. She really wanted the barn to get some more use, see some new riders, and I would've helped with that and worked on my art. Done some pet sitting. There is definitely some space for it, and animals are—"

"Often better than people," Leah and Madison echoed.

They shared a quick grin, eyes twinkling in the reflected bar light before Madison shook her head. "Wow. Why law school, if that was on offer?"

Leah sighed, looking away. "After the relationship my mom warned me about blew up in my face, I thought I should go back to following her advice. It would've been a difficult way to make a living, anyway. So, law school, and here we are."

Madison echoed her sigh. "Here we are."

Sinking into the couch the following evening, Leah took a deep breath in and released a drawn-out "fffffuuuuuuuck" on the exhale. Grabbing her phone, she shot off a quick text to her cousin, Cassidy.

> My job sucks. Something came up that I should have known about but didn't. Why is life so much?

After dropping the phone back to the couch, Leah grabbed the remote and started where she had left off in her latest rewatch of *Leverage*. If she were more responsible, she'd try to sleep. But she wasn't, and she was too revved from the day to make the attempt.

Cassidy's response came through quickly.

> Girl, you have got to find a different job.

Leah wrinkled her nose, sticking her tongue out at the phone before shooting back her response.

> But, money.

Leah could clearly picture the look of exasperation on Cassidy's face when she typed the rejoinder.

> But mental health.

Leah stared at her screen, not sure how to respond. She laughed softly to herself, eyes tearing when her phone lit up with the picture of the two of them at Valley Scare, toasting each other with a turkey leg and cotton candy.

When Leah answered, Cassidy picked up right where they left off, "Lee, c'mon, this job is killing you. Why not quit?"

Leah rubbed her eyes, trying to ignore the panicky feeling in her chest. She wanted to quit, but she didn't know what was next, and she absolutely refused to move forward without a plan. It was beyond risky, and she didn't do risky. Not anymore.

Leah couldn't hide her exhaustion when she responded, "What would I do, Cassidy?"

Cassidy's sigh carried clearly through the phone line. No doubt she was at least a little annoyed at rehashing the same conversation, but she was the one who brought it up. Of course, Leah had been the one to open this line of communication with her first text, but that was beside the point she was trying to make...to herself.

"Literally anything else, girl. Don't tell me you haven't thought about other career paths that would work. Sell your art, for one. Do the festival circuit you've always dreamed about."

Leah sighed deeply, leaning back against her couch and closing her eyes. "I couldn't afford to live off artwork alone. I'm not good enough."

Cassidy scoffed. "Well, you can't know until you try, and I say you are absolutely good enough. Maybe not enough to afford the crazy city rates you're paying, but you hate it there anyway. Move somewhere cheaper, dip into your savings, live a little."

Leah frowned at the idea of dipping into her retirement or emergency savings. Neither pool of money was for risk-taking. "Ew, gross, no."

"Which part? Living a little?" Cassidy snorted. "Fair. I can see how living might feel weird to you with all this surviving you've been doing instead."

Leah let out a fake gasp of outrage. "You're going to come at me like this? In my own home? You dare?"

Cassidy laughed. "I dare. I vote it's time you shake up your life and get the hell out of Dodge. Dip your toe into your savings. It's not like you can't live on next to nothing, anyway. Worst case, everything falls apart terribly, and you move back in with Sadie as you had planned."

She was too tired for this conversation. Choosing to go with the quickest way to stop Cassidy's pushing, Leah asked, "What, you're not going to offer your place?"

"Hey, if you want to squeeze into my closet, you're welcome."

"Luxury living," Leah murmured, laughter coating her voice.

"You know it. But seriously, Lee, at least promise me you'll think about it. Really, actually consider it."

Leah could practically feel Cassidy's worry through the line. Wanting to ease her mind but with no intention of actually following through, she agreed.

Cassidy was silent for a while before she sighed. "Look, if you're not going to really think about it, at least gather some more information. Talk to Sadie about your old plans for the place, see if she still wants to do it. You told me the fires were mostly out at work, and nothing big needed to be done before next week, right?"

"Yeah," Leah agreed cautiously.

"Great, take Friday off and go talk this through with Aunt Sadie. I'm sure she'd be thrilled, even if it doesn't end up going anywhere. If nothing else, you'll spend a long weekend where it's so much harder for your to-do list to haunt you. Your clients won't be able to track you down, and neither will the partners."

Taking a deep breath in, Leah allowed herself to actually think it through. Running through her mental list of files and the pending to-do list, she nodded to herself. "Okay."

"Okay, really?" Cassidy asked, suspicion coating her voice.

Leah laughed. "Yes, really."

"Excellent," Cassidy said. "Then I am getting off the phone before you try to wheedle your way back out of it."

"Fine, be that way."

When Cassidy laughed at her over-the-top pouty voice, Leah grinned, snuggling back down on the couch. She loved the sound of her cousin's laugh. "Thanks, Cass."

"Anytime, boo. Now hop to it on the follow-through."

Rolling her eyes, Leah murmured, "Yes, ma'am."

After exchanging goodbyes, Leah hung up. Before she chickened out, she pulled up her calendar to make sure she hadn't forgotten anything for Friday. Finding nothing on the schedule and nothing the following Monday, she marked herself out for the weekend.

Chapter Two: Unmoored

Leah jerked awake two weeks later, hand automatically reaching to turn off her alarm, only to find her alarm wasn't going off. She squinted blearily at her screen reflecting an Unknown Caller beneath the 3:00AM display. No good calls happened at 3:00 once you were past twenty-eight.

Quickly swiping her finger to answer the call, she rasped an inquiring hello.

Confusion almost overtook the panic as the voice she had tried for years to forget sounded from the other end of the line. "Leah, your aunt's in the hospital. You need to get here."

She shot up in bed, hand moving to cover her rapidly beating heart as panic coursed through her. "What happened?"

"It's her heart," Liam said tersely. "It doesn't look good. Call this number when you get to the hospital."

He hung up after her quick agreement, and Leah half fell out of the bed in her haste to get to her aunt's side. Stumbling across the room, she pulled on the nearest pants she could find. She grabbed her purse on the way out the door and raced down to the apartment garage.

The miles between her apartment and Clearwater passed in a blur. The fact that she'd be seeing her ex for the first time in years was overwhelmed by the sheer panic roaring through her. After parking haphazardly in the nearly empty hospital lot, she tapped the most recent number, pushing herself out of her car and jogging toward the hospital as the ringtone filled her ear.

After picking up, Liam directed her to the intensive care unit on the third floor of the hospital. Leah rushed to the elevators, pushing her phone back into her purse on the way. As she waited for the elevator to reach her floor, she bounced her hand against her thigh, continuing the motion as she entered the elevator and waited for it to deposit her on the third floor. Why was everything taking so long?

Time crawled as the elevator ticked through the floors. After an eternity, the doors opened, and she hustled to the ICU's nurses' station. When the nurse at the desk looked up at her, Leah blurted, "Sadie Carter? I was told she's here. I'm her niece, Leah."

The older woman nodded, typing the information into her computer before pointing to the room directly behind the desk. "The doctor is with her now. Room 3-49."

Leah rushed out a quick "thank you" before scurrying to the indicated room. She immediately spotted Liam leaning against the wall with his arms crossed, watching the nurse like a hawk as he checked Sadie's vitals.

The doctor turned from the computer and gave Leah a tight smile. "Ms. Carter?"

Leah nodded sharply, wrapping her arms around her own waist. She tried to hold herself together. The rapid beating of her heart told her she was seconds away from shattering into a million pieces.

"Mr. Devlin told me you were on the way. I'm Dr. Gatewell, and this is Dominic. We've been taking care of your aunt since she was admitted to the hospital. Would you like to step out, so we can speak privately?"

Before Leah could answer, Liam's deep voice rang out, "I'll go." Looking over to Leah, he raised a single eyebrow before asking, "Text me?"

"I will," she agreed shakily, staring at Sadie. Her larger-than-life aunt looked pale and small in the hospital bed. She barely noticed Liam leaving the room.

Blinking back tears, Leah turned to Dr. Gatewell. "What happened?"

Dr. Gatewell's expression was the almost detached sympathy of a professional who had already seen and dealt with too much in her career. She spoke softly when she answered, "I'm afraid your aunt suffered a massive heart attack. I understand Mr. Devlin found her at her farm a few hours ago. He brought her to the hospital."

Leah tightened her arms around her body. Cold overtook her. "Will she be alright? Please tell me she's going to be okay. People recover from heart attacks all the time, don't they?" She absently noticed an edge of hysteria creeping into her voice.

The doctor's voice was maddeningly understanding and sympathetic. "I'm sorry, but we won't know that for a while yet. Tonight will be critical to her recovery. I don't want you to lose hope, but I'm not going to sugarcoat anything. It doesn't look good. If she makes it through the next few days, she'll have a long recovery ahead of her."

Leah's breath stuttered. It felt like she was trying to breathe through a straw while her heart battled to escape her chest. As tears started trickling down her face, she forced herself to take a deep breath. She needed information. She wouldn't get it by giving in to the screaming panic.

"What do we do in the meantime? Did you explain all of this to..." Unable to get the last word out, she gestured at the door to indicate Liam.

"He may have overheard several things in the emergency room, but no. I'm sure he would appreciate an update. Only if you and your aunt would be comfortable with you sharing the information, of course."

Leah nodded, wiping the tears from her face. "Do you need anything else from me? Sadie told me she had her health care directive on file already, but I think I can get another original, if you need one."

Dr. Gatewell nodded sharply, giving her a small smile. "It's on file along with a copy of your driver's license. They may want a new copy of your license, but it's not something you need to worry about right now."

She logged off the computer and angled toward the door. "I have to see to other patients now. Dominic is the nurse assigned to your aunt. He'll let you know before he leaves for the day. Please don't hesitate to let him know if you have any other questions."

Leah moved to her aunt's side, hesitantly taking Sadie's hand in her own. "Can she..." Her voice broke before she could finish the question. She inhaled a shuddery breath. She could do this. She could ask a simple question.

Dominic answered before she pulled herself together. "I believe she can hear you. She's not in any pain right now. There's a chair right behind you. Not the most comfortable, but it serves its purpose."

Leah gave him a weak smile and forced out a thank you.

Dominic gave her a soft smile in return and gestured at the call button. "Push that if you need anything. We're only a few steps away."

Before she could thank him again, he strode out of the room, the door closing silently behind him.

When she turned to Sadie, the sobs she had been holding back burst out of her. Gasping for air, she knelt by the bed and clasped Sadie's hand between hers. Shivers overtook her as her body attempted to dispel the bone-deep cold.

Leah stared at her reflection numbly as she let the cool water she'd just pressed against her face fall back into the sink. Her blue eyes were rimmed with red. The brown hair framing her face was damp and ruffled from sleep and stress. She shook her hands off before wiping them on a towel. At least the anxiety attack, one of an ever-increasing number, had a silver lining. She was comfortably numb now. After flicking off the bathroom light, she made her way back to Sadie's side.

The chair scraped against the linoleum as she pulled it to Sadie's bedside. She shuddered as the sound sent a shiver down her spine. Shaking it off, she sat, making the chair squeak. Finding a position that was comfortable enough to tolerate, she began tracing her fingers up and down Sadie's arm.

"Remember when you used to do this for me? This and your hot cocoa remain the superior method of dealing with heartbreak and stress. Cashing in one of those homemade coupons would have been an easier way to get me to do this for you, but you always were one for overkill."

She huffed out a quick breath, scrubbing her hands over her face before stretching her fingers out in front of her. Her skin felt too tight. Physical discomfort was a small price to pay for the fuzzy cloud that settled over her post-anxiety attack.

She breathed slowly, trying to organize her thoughts. What did she need to do? Right. Her cousins. They needed to know. They should get here. Just in case... Just in case.

Pulling her phone out of her pocket, she was momentarily distracted by the minute trembling of her hand. Adrenaline. Right. She shook her head at herself before focusing again on her breath. In for a count of four, hold for a count of four, exhale for a count of four. Rinse and repeat.

Breathing out the last shaky exhale, she pulled up the group chat she had with her cousins. Cassidy, Paige, Derek, and Leah had all spent almost every summer of their childhood at Sadie's farm. She could almost hear the echo of their laughter and the crackle of bonfires.

> Sadie is in the hospital, and it doesn't sound good.

> We won't know how bad it is until the morning, but the doctors are sure she had a massive heart attack.

> Liam brought her into the hospital. I'm here with her now. If you can make it, I think you should come.

Setting her phone down on the bed, she focused back on Sadie. "I'm not sure what you know about the sequence of events that brought us here." She blinked at the robotic tone of her voice.

"That didn't sound creepy at all. Anyway, Liam found you. Brought you to the hospital and called me. My first boyfriend calling me at ass o'clock in the morning was *not* on this year's bingo card."

After grabbing her phone, she pulled up the last number dialed. She buried a groan at the thought of voluntarily reaching out to him. She wasn't going to back out on her promise, especially not after he called her in the first place.

> Heart attack. They'll know more prognosis-wise in the morning.

"He wanted an update. Which is fair, you know. Given you decided to terrify all of the people who care about you. I suppose you'd want me to invite him to come visit, too, huh? You're all about that grace."

> If you want to come by when the hospital opens up again for visitors, I can make myself scarce.

She searched her aunt's still face for any reaction. Finding nothing, she released a shaky exhale. "Alright, he's invited. I'm not sticking around though, so if you have any ideas about some sort of second chance romance, I would suggest leaving that to the romance novels."

> I'll be there.

Dropping her head back against the chair, Leah muttered, "He at least could have gotten ugly."

Chapter Three: In Her Wake

Cassidy bumped her shoulder against Leah's. She was looking toward the door of the funeral home with a grimace. "Need me to stick around until he's gone?"

Leah sighed heavily at the sight of Liam Devlin's tall frame coming through the door of the reception room. She hadn't seen him since the morning Sadie died. Black slacks hugged his long legs. The sleeves of his white dress shirt were rolled up to his elbows. He had filled out in ways Leah hadn't noticed in the hospital. His forearms were corded with lean muscle, and his shoulders were broader than she remembered. And, of fucking course, one lock of his dark hair fell forward into his eye. What did she do in a past life to deserve this?

She sighed. It would be fine. Glancing back at Cassidy, she shook her head. "No, I can be an adult about this. We're not teenagers anymore. I'm sure we can be cordial."

"Eh," Cassidy replied, "I'm sure you can be. Not so sure about junior over there."

"You might be giving me too much credit." Leah smiled at Cassidy's muffled bark of laughter. The other woman shoved her shoulder, eyes twinkling.

"This is the kind of thing Sadie would've wanted."

"What, watching the torture of me talking to my ex?"

Cassidy rolled her eyes. "No, you doofus. Laughter."

Leah smiled softly. "Yeah, she would've liked that." She looked around at the somber attendees. Hushed voices filled the room with a low drone of sound. "Too bad it's simply not about her."

Per the funeral home director's suggestion, they were spread throughout the receiving room to allow for a slightly more natural atmosphere. On the bright side, it allowed people who didn't actually know Leah but knew other relatives to skip her. On the other hand, she had more relatives than she remembered and recognized only a handful of them. If they hadn't agreed to divide and conquer, she could've leaned on her parents' memory of all of the names. The lecture about respect and remembering names might even have been worth it.

In deference to the location, Cassidy managed to smother her laughter at Leah's droll reply, but her eyes danced with her amusement. "If you're sure, I'm going to go rescue Derek. Give me a signal if you change your mind and need your own rescue."

"I'll be sure to send up a nice signal flare," Leah said.

"Perfect," Cassidy said with a wink. "I shouldn't miss that."

Leah watched Cassidy's slow progress to Derek until Liam reached her side. She masked her sigh with a deep breath before turning to him. "Liam," she murmured, "thanks for coming."

Ducking his head in acknowledgment, he slid his hands into his pockets. "Of course. Sadie was good to me."

She smiled tightly. As if she hadn't been good to him. Leah bit back a sigh at the familiar course of irritation running through her. Of course, her post-anxiety attack numbness would finish wearing off now. She was not going to go off on him at Sadie's funeral. Sadie might have ultimately gotten a kick out of it, but the rest of the family would not be amused. And why was she even irritated about this? Sadie *was* good to him. She was good to a lot of people.

"Listen, I'm taking care of the horses because Sadie asked me to step up in case anything happened to her."

Leah blinked at the abrupt statement. "Right," she said, nodding slowly. "We all really appreciate it, thank you."

He looked away from her, casting his gaze out across the room full of people mourning Sadie.

Looking back at her, he moved his hand through the air as if to wave away the gratitude. "I'm doing it for Sadie, not any of you. You need to figure something out for them. I'm not going to keep doing this forever."

"Right," Leah cleared her throat, "of course not. I was wondering whether you knew of any rescues in the area that could take them on. Or if you knew whether Sadie had been looking."

Liam rolled his eyes, a muscle in his jaw ticking. "I got Cassidy's message. I don't know of any rescues who would want to step into the mess that is Athena and Hermes. I assume, between the collective degrees the four of you have managed to acquire, you can figure it out within the next couple weeks."

She clenched her jaw. She had forgotten how hard his condescension could hit. "I don't know what a degree in anything has to do with local connections to rescue groups, but sure. Thanks anyway."

"So, two weeks?"

"Right," she bit out, "two weeks." She held back the urge to ask him if his bill would be in the mail. Knowing him, he would tell her it was, charge a ridiculous rate, and tack on a pain-in-the-ass surcharge. All spelled out, of course.

When Liam turned to walk away, she called him back, a thought coming to her. At his clear impatience and raised eyebrow, she shrugged before mumbling a false apology.

When he crossed his arms, she shot him an insincere smile. "While you're here, since you'll be done helping with Sadie's animals, you'll have all of your stuff off the farm by the end of the two weeks, right?"

His eyebrows flicked up in surprise before he scoffed, irritation sparking in his eyes. "Sure, Lee, I'll have my stuff off the farm in two weeks."

He started to turn away again before snapping his fingers and looking back at her. "I won't have the time to take care of the ditches, though. It's a bit overgrown out there, and you know how the county can get about things not being taken care of by the beginning of June."

Her mouth dropped open, surprise coursing through her. "It's not done yet?"

He shook his head slowly, mockingly. "'Fraid not," he said with a click of his tongue. "Might want to get on that before you're looking down the barrel of a citation."

He winked before sauntering away to the photo displays. She drew in a slow breath, trying to tamp down the absolute fury rising in her chest. She was overreacting. It was probably the grief. She took a deep breath. She would not cause a scene.

She started toward him before a hand on her arm made her jump with a muffled yelp.

"Jesus. What?" she snapped. Paige still held her arm in a tight grip.

Paige released her, relaxing her grip one finger at a time, after Leah looked pointedly at the hand digging into her arm. Taking a step back, Paige raised her hands. "You okay?"

Leah crossed her arms, grinding her teeth together briefly as she tried to get herself under control. "I'm fine."

"Okay," Paige said slowly, "you don't look fine. You look like you want to murder Liam."

"Yes, well, Liam is a prick. We have a deadline to figure something out with the horses, figure out how we're going to take care of Grayson when he's only ever lived on a farm, and somehow get the goddamn grass cut when it's tall enough to make hay bales because Liam didn't bother to get that done."

"Ah," Paige murmured, "I see. I'm sure we can get it all figured out. Liam was probably dealing with a lot. Maybe we can hire Liam to take care of the grass? He did it for Sadie for free, but we don't have that relationship."

"Ha, yeah," Leah bit out, crossing her arms. "No way in hell I'm paying that man to do anything. He threatened to report us to the county."

"Whoa, easy there, Lee. No need to have a temper tantrum."

Leah opened her mouth to defend herself, eyes tight with anger. Paige held up a hand. "Nope, I'm not doing this with you. I don't know what he said, and I don't care. We're all dealing with losing Sadie, and I don't appreciate you adding to my pile."

Leah flinched, mentally cursing out Liam for fraying her already worn emotions. She took a breath, pushing her anger down into a box before looking back at Paige. "I'm sorry, Paige. I thought he was done getting to me like this."

Paige nodded. "Okay, apology accepted. Don't let it happen again."

Leah nodded, face flaming. She was too old to be called out like this. Hell, Paige would tell her she was too old to act like this.

"Right. You're right." Trying to add in some humor, she said, "Hey, on the bright side, there is now a timeline for how long I need to tolerate his bullshit."

"Okay, clearly we're not being reasonable today," Paige muttered. "You should duck into the side room and get some food, take a breath."

Based on the expression on Paige's face, Leah wouldn't get anywhere trying to tell Paige she was simply trying to lighten the mood. Paige was at the end of her patience. She reminded herself that she was not the only one reeling. Just because Sadie processed her negative emotions with the occasional dark joke did not mean Paige would appreciate them.

Instead, she agreed and thanked the other woman for the suggestion.

"You're welcome, princess," Paige said with a smug grin.

Right. Paige was the only one allowed to make shitty jokes. Choosing to ignore the childhood taunt, Leah walked away. She hoped desperately there was something sweet in the family room. She needed to eat her feelings stat.

She raised her eyebrows at the sight of Cassidy and Derek at the little round table crammed into the family room. They were each eating a bowl of ice cream. Hopefully, they had some more.

At their slightly guilty expressions, she grinned. "You beat me to it. Is there any more?"

They both pointed to the little freezer almost hidden beneath the counter on the opposite side of the room. She nodded sharply and grabbed a bowl. Joining them at the table, she set down her bowl with a little clatter. "This sucks," she muttered, voice cracking.

Staring into their own bowls, Derek and Cassidy nodded silently. She took a scoop of ice cream, letting it melt in her mouth while she wiped away the traitorous tears. She didn't give them permission to escape.

Except for the clink of spoons, the room was silent for several minutes until Derek cleared his throat. "You can break the tie. Ice cream. Appropriate to eat at a wake or no?"

Leah shrugged before arching an eyebrow. "Do we care?"

Cassidy cast her a watery grin. "Derek would like to know if he's being a little rebel or not."

He rolled his eyes at his sister's jab. "I'm not sure we really care, but now that Cass and I started an argument about it, I'd like additional opinions."

"Eh," Leah said, waffling her hand back and forth, "definitely not traditional. Miss Manners would probably say it's not appropriate, but the non-existent Self-Care Susan would say whatever helps you cope with the shit show going on around you is appropriate."

Cassidy's voice was muffled from the spoonful of ice cream she'd just popped into her mouth. "Self-Care Susan is my favorite imaginary bitch."

"Mine too," Leah agreed.

Derek nodded. "She's good people."

Chapter Four: Picking Up the Pieces

Leah bounced her head against the steering wheel, groaning. Sadie had left her the farm, dividing the personal property and cash among the cousins. The catch? The farm was over-mortgaged. While it wasn't underwater, refinancing would require more cash up front. A lot of cash.

She should sell the farm, pocket a little cash, and move on with her life. It was too far from work. The upkeep alone would require weekends she didn't have. And who in their right mind would dive into a pool of debt that deep? And yet... It was *Sadie's farm*. Her escape. Her home.

Leaning back against the seat, she stared up the long drive. She'd leave the car here. Walk up it. Use the time to clear her head. If she had any good luck hanging out there, she'd convince herself to take the reasonable path.

Good luck was clearly not on her side today. The checklist for preparing the place for sale did not pop up in her mind on the long walk. Instead, she was bombarded with thoughts of her firm's sabbatical policy and her accrued vacation. You weren't meant to make major life decisions within six months of a major loss anyway.

When the farm came into view, Leah gasped. She usually felt immense peace at this view. Now, pain shot through her. She rubbed her sternum, trying to rub away the phantom pain. It felt like someone was carving a hole in her chest with a rusty spoon. Leah half-sat, half-collapsed onto the gravel with a shuddering gasp. She'd never see Sadie again. No more late-night bitch sessions over mugs of hot cocoa. She'd never again feel Sadie's arms wrap around her, sheltering her from the pain of the world.

A soft woof broke her out of the spiral. Grayson, Sadie's Great Pyrenees, was trotting up to her. When he pushed his big head into her shoulder, she buried her face in his soft fur. She wept. For everything she had taken for granted. The meals and holidays she'd never again share with Sadie. The unconditional acceptance of everything she was and everything she could be.

When she sat up, she wasn't sure how long she'd been there wrapped around Grayson. Standing, she kept a hand buried in Grayson's fur. She barely took in the historic farmhouse, the large barn, or Sadie's tiny house sheltered by a small copse of trees. Everything seemed dull, lacking the vibrant colors she remembered.

The bright red of the barn with its beautifully contrasting white trim looked washed out. As if the red had somehow faded in the days since she was last here. The grand porch of the farmhouse looked colder. The familiar echo of past laughter, bonfires, and sticky s'mores, consumed while racing between the porch and the fire pit, was just...gone.

Leah gazed blankly at the hayloft, expecting the typical rush of irritating memories of days long since passed. No matter how many times she'd been out to visit Sadie, she had always, always had flashes of her and Liam. Sharing a picnic in the hayloft, giggling as they shared secrets and swapped ghost stories. Kissing with the loft doors open for a view of the stars. Going further when they were sure no one was around to catch them. Now, nothing. The absence of the rush of memories that had aggravated her so much now left her feeling empty.

Walking up the porch steps, Leah numbly dug out the keys before letting herself into the farmhouse foyer, barely noticing Grayson staying on the porch. Numbly, she toed her shoes off out of respect for the woman who wasn't here to receive it. In a daze, she made her way into the front family room.

Sinking into one of the armchairs, Leah stared at the empty fireplace. Her gaze blurred, pushing the grate and pile of ashes out of focus as she just... stopped. Stopped trying to be okay.

Leah snapped back into focus with a start, shivering. The room was significantly dimmer and cooler than when she had entered. She absentmindedly wiped the tears off her face before standing, immediately needing to catch herself against the chair when her legs didn't respond as expected. When she felt stable enough, she moved toward the front door, legs tingling.

Stepping onto the porch after shoving her cold feet back into her shoes, she smiled softly at the familiar sight of Grayson watching over his domain. His tail thumped solidly against the wood floor at the sight of her. Locking the door behind her, she considered retrieving her car. Complete and utter exhaustion won. It would be fine.

Grayson followed her to the steps of Sadie's little cabin. She stared at the door silently. Keys. Right. She needed to get out the keys, so she could unlock the door. Pushing her hand into her pocket, she startled at the sharp bite of keys against her palm. Opening her hand, she blinked down at it stupidly. The keys were still in her hand.

She didn't know how long she stared before Grayson nosed her hand, snapping her out of her funk. Sighing raggedly, she pushed the appropriate key into the lock of Sadie's door. When Grayson followed her inside, she sagged with relief. She didn't want to be alone.

She spared a brief glance for Sadie's bedroom door before pushing her way into the second bedroom. It had been hers for the end of her high school career. And then Liam's after Leah left for college. He had been couch-surfing since his father kicked him out the day he turned eighteen. Once the room was available again, Sadie had welcomed him into her home. It had taken weeks, and a long conversation with Sadie, for Leah to process the feelings it had caused.

Liam moved out before the summer of their freshman year, and Leah had made the space hers again. She barely glanced at the familiar walls before kicking her shoes off and collapsing face down onto the bed. Figuring things out could wait until tomorrow. Maybe Rosalee, Sadie's best friend and a strong mentor to Leah since Leah was old enough to speak in complete sentences, could talk some sense into her. She sighed, snuggling down into the pillows when Grayson jumped onto the bed. She fell asleep with his giant head on her back.

Leah stared at Rosalee, sitting calmly across from her as if she hadn't just dropped an emotional bomb in her lap. "You were... You were supposed to talk me out of this cockamamie idea, not *into it*."

"Oh," Rosalee asked innocently, her golden-brown hands wrapped loosely around her mug of tea, "was that what I was supposed to do? I'm sorry, dear, I didn't get that memo."

Leah closed her mouth before taking another sip from her own cup, mind whirring.

Rosalee shamelessly used her silence to push her own agenda. The traitor. "You love this place, Lee, and I know you and your aunt had some plans for making everything cash flow."

"We did, but it would take so much more than we planned with the refinancing, and she isn't..." She released a shaky exhale. "She isn't *here*, Ros. I don't know how to do this without her. I don't have her connections, or her experience."

"Connections, I can manage, honey. But I need to know what you want, Leah. What do you really want?"

"I want to stay," she blurted. "I want to see through what Sadie wanted to do with this place. The boarding. Opening the trails. Hosting lessons. See it come alive like when she and her husband started this place."

Rosalee hummed. "We can do that, honey. But be careful you aren't trading one frying pan for another."

Leah sighed, scrubbing a hand across her face. "I don't know what you mean."

"Sadie made it fairly clear how little you like the job you have now. It's also been abundantly clear how much you love working on your art out here. I couldn't help but notice you didn't mention that at all in your list there."

"I love working on the wood-burning, but that isn't going to turn a livable profit anytime soon. Definitely not soon enough to refinance this farm. And especially not enough to handle the mortgage payments. It's already impractical to try to make it work as a boarding facility on such short notice. I'm crazy to even be considering it, and I'm still not sure where your rational businesswoman brain went."

When Ros arched an eyebrow, Leah pushed her lip out in a fake pout. "I was counting on you to tell me this is crazy, and I should sell the farm."

Ros laughed, eyes crinkling with her amusement. "I may be a little biased, but you love this place, Leah. I can't see you being happy with letting it go and walking away. You can make this happen. You're smart, and you're resourceful, and I'll do everything I can to help you see this through. But I don't want to see you stuck doing something you don't want to do. Sadie wouldn't have wanted that."

Leah stared into the woods, poking at her motivation. Was she trading one set of problems for another?

"Yeah," she finally said, shaking her head in disbelief. "I want this farm, Ros. If nothing else, the view is certainly better. Trying to make art my main source of income is a no-go, though."

"Alright. I'll help you make this place a good bet for any mortgage company worth its salt." She held up a hand before Leah could thank her. "On two conditions. First, you promise me you'll commit to spending time on your art every day. I don't care if it's five minutes or five hours. You'll do it every day."

She held Leah's gaze until Leah nodded.

"Good. Second, you'll meet with Tasha like Sadie wanted. Or send her your portfolio or whatever it is Sadie had arranged between the two of you. Sadie had high hopes for seeing your art take off after Tasha's gallery show coming up this season."

Leah bit her lip. The last thing she wanted to do while she was already feeling fragile was open herself up to more rejection. Studying the firm set to Ros's features, she groaned. Clearly, this was non-negotiable, and she wasn't going to convince Ros that the art wasn't worth the time it'd take. She had pieces already finished, cluttering up the studio. She could send photos to Tasha, and she could surely spare five minutes every day.

"You drive a hard bargain." She laughed at Ros's wink. "Alright, agreed. Thank you, seriously. I don't know what'd I do if I lost you and Sadie both."

"Fortunately for the both of us, you don't have to figure that out. Where do you want to start?"

Leah looked around the property, processing her options. "People who want somewhere to board. Trainers who don't have a local barn yet or want another space. That would be a good draw for boarding leased horses here. And the trails.

"We can market the trails as coming soon. The fact that they lead straight into the state land should be a good selling point."

When she looked back to Rosalee, the other woman was smiling warmly. "You got it. Now about Hermes and Athena."

Leah groaned and buried her face in her hands. Athena and Hermes. They were old, cranky, and didn't much care for any other horses being anywhere near their space. They didn't particularly care for most people, either.

"I feel bad for looking for a rescue to take them on."

Ros cocked her head to the side, her brow furrowing. "Why would you be looking?"

Leah blushed furiously. "It's just... I love them, but they..." She waved her hands at a loss for words until Ros stopped her, eyes dancing.

"No, sweetheart. Sadie agreed with you. They were getting to be too much, and she'd already gone into debt getting them back to this point of healthy. She had a rescue lined up. I think they're supposed to be here by the end of the month. Possibly by the end of the season." She shrugged, expression wry. "Sadie and I didn't deal a whole lot in the details."

Leah's eyes widened, shock coursing through her. "You're kidding."

"Not at all. I only brought them up in case you were thinking you should keep them. I was going to do my best to talk you out of it. It took Sadie months to track down a place that was willing and able to take them."

When Leah continued to study her, gobsmacked, Ros laughed. "You should see the goats that are going to be their future roommates. Alyssa, she's the owner of the rescue, brought out a few a couple months back to make sure Hermes and Athena would acclimate to them. Got along like a house on fire; it was adorable. I'll send you the information I have, so you can coordinate the retrieval."

Leah nodded, feeling a bit numb. Irritation quickly chased away the shock when she remembered her conversation with Liam. That little shit.

"Did Liam know about Alyssa?"

Rosalee pursed her lips, thinking. "I can't imagine he didn't know. He was out here helping Sadie with one thing or another all of the time, and the goats were here quite a while."

"Wait, yes. He definitely knew. He drove Sadie out to Alyssa's place, so she could get a tour. See the facilities and where the horses would be staying. Why do you ask?"

Leah drew in a deep breath and released it slowly. "Because we asked Liam if he had any potential leads on re-homing the horses. Twice. And he said no."

Rosalee burst out laughing at the news, laughing harder when Leah frowned at her.

"Honey, I'm sorry," she said, holding up a placating hand, "but I cannot believe the two of you are still trying to get under the other's skin."

Leah's mouth dropped open. "Hey, what do you mean the *two* of us? I haven't done anything to him."

Rosalee tried and failed to suppress a snort at the question. "Are you seriously telling me you've done absolutely nothing to get under his skin? Not a single thing?"

Leah bit her lip. "He started it." She noted with no small amount of consternation that her own tone was petulant. She had clearly regressed.

She cast Ros a wounded expression, and the other woman burst out into new peals of laughter. The sight of tears tracking down the other woman's face due to the force of her laughter triggered Leah's own set of giggles. She bent over the table, holding her stomach, as she laughed. Maybe, just maybe, it would all turn out okay.

Chapter Five: Treading Water

Leah released a tired puff of air, pushing a sweaty strand of hair out of her eyes. Weeks after her conversation with Ros, she still had doubts. Fortunately, her firm had agreed to a modified sabbatical plan. She had time to figure things out. Unfortunately, the time left her frequently turning over options in her mind. She couldn't sleep, but she was too tired to work on her latest piece. Rather than continue tossing and turning, she'd come out to the barn.

Sadie had a hard time letting go of anything, a trait shared by many members of her family. Leah had worked up a sweat sorting out the boxes that belonged to various family members. The things Sadie had stored for her friends had already been retrieved in the weeks since her death. Knowing her family would take longer to pick up their things, despite her request to have the barn emptied, she had started stacking their boxes into empty stalls.

Leah suspected a genetic component at play. The Carter Family Weakness ™ was a susceptibility to hoarding-like tendencies. She snorted at herself, earning a look from Grayson. She blew him a raspberry. "You should be accustomed to crazy Carters."

He released a soft boof and laid his head down on his paws, continuing to study her. She returned her attention to the boxes filled with Sadie's stuff. She was impressed. Sadie had held on to less than she had expected. It was still a lot, no question, but the majority of the mess had been more about Sadie's helpful nature than her inability to let go.

Looking over the space, she frowned at Liam's car. True to his word, he'd stopped taking care of the horses two weeks ago. She wouldn't admit it to him, but the two weeks had been a godsend. It was enough time for Leah to get her caseload under control or handed off in preparation for her semi-sabbatical.

Despite stopping his care of the horses, Liam had not removed his freaking car. She rolled her eyes. It wasn't a big deal, and she didn't need to make it one. She absolutely did not need to draw him into some sort of war over the car. She had enough on her plate as it was. She'd call him tomorrow, remind him to get the car out before her meeting with Ros's first round of potential business partners.

She stuck her tongue out at the car. She'd text him instead. She didn't want to hear his voice. Plan in place, she returned to the last stack of Paige's boxes. Paige's name, heart over the I on each label, stood out in bold purple lettering. She grinned. Paige had consistently claimed she didn't have that much stuff at Sadie's.

Turned out, she had the most. The remaining boxes were small, relatively light, but oddly shaped. She *should* carry them out in two trips. But she didn't want to make the extra trip. She was ready for bed. She was ready to be done with this project.

She squatted down, securely grasping the bottom box and lifting with her legs. She stood slowly, maneuvering the boxes to lean securely against her. She could barely see, but she knew the way well after the thousand trips she'd already taken out of the arena. She grinned as she started the slow route to the stall. Clearly, one trip was the right call. She totally had this.

As her foot caught on something, she had enough time to realize she did not in fact have this before she fell sideways. Her hip smashed into something hard. When her right arm smacked against the same thing, she dropped the boxes with a curse. As they fell, two of the boxes smacked into her knee before clattering to the ground.

She yelped, trying to grasp her knee and immediately toppling sideways. Her ribs glanced off another box before she fell beside it on the ground. Curling into the fetal position, she cursed, tears filling her eyes. She lay there for several beats, absently noting when Grayson trotted over to her side. Laying on the ground, she slowly catalogued her limbs before patting Grayson's big head.

Yeah, she definitely didn't have that. Pushing herself into a seated position, she felt along her ribs, wondering how she'd be able to tell whether she broke anything. They certainly hurt enough, but she wasn't feeling anything move. Looking down at her knee, she laughed at the sight of the large red mark. Oh, good. She only sounded a little unhinged. Yeah, that was going to bruise spectacularly. Wonderful. Just wonderful.

She spared a moment to assure Grayson that all was well before twisting to her right to see what she had fallen into. Her mouth dropped open. Liam's *fucking* car. She smacked the door with her palm, cursing when a new bark of pain spread down her arm. *So helpful, Leah.* She scowled. Shaking her hand out, she released a heavy sigh.

Okay. This was fine. It was not actually his fault. She knew the car was there. Of course, had he moved it by the deadline *he had set*, she wouldn't have fallen into it. She could've corrected her balance and been absolutely fine. Nope. She wasn't going to do this. She wasn't going to blame him for a simple mistake. This was not the path of a rational adult, years post-breakup.

She scrubbed her face and pushed her hands back through her hair. Next steps. Figure out what made her trip. Avoid a repeat. She should move whatever it was out of the way. She hadn't noticed any obstacles as she carried out the rest of the boxes.

Spotting the culprit, her eyes widened and her mouth dropped open for the second time in as many minutes. What the ever-loving hell? *That asshole.* He left a jack underneath the car, the lever creating a subtle tripping hazard she hadn't spotted. She'd been giving the car a wide berth in the hopes of not sparking additional anger, so of course it hadn't been a problem until her vision was obscured.

That's it, she told herself, pushing herself up into a standing position before dusting herself off. *That car is out of here.*

Leah dropped the dish she was washing with a startled curse when loud knocking cut through her music. She pushed a damp hand against her chest. Her heart rate had jumped at the unexpected noise. She bit her lip lightly before answering the door. Whoever was on the other side sounded pissed. When another round of banging rang out, her eyes darted to the baseball bat she kept next to the door. She grasped it lightly in her left hand, hiding it behind the door as she opened it.

Liam's fist was raised to knock again, his mouth drawn down in a furious scowl. *Shit.* The car. How had she forgotten about the car? She'd had it towed in a spurt of rage. Falling into the thing had been the last straw. First, lying to her about the rescue. Then, she'd received a warning from the county about the grass.

The warning noted she'd need to get the grass in shape by the end of the week. They only sent out a warning this early when someone complained. And there was only one person who would make the complaint about Sadie's place so soon after she had died. All of her good intentions to not engage with him blew out the window after she tripped over the stupid handle of the jack, sticking out like a tripwire.

Maybe...they hadn't been out yet to tow it. Maybe he was just mad about something completely unrelated. Totally possible.

"Can I help you?" she asked, forcing a bright tone.

He took a breath, eyes narrowing as he crossed his arms, forearms flexing. "Where. Is. My. Fucking. Car. Leah," he bit out slowly.

Yeah, the car not being towed was about as likely as pigs flying. He didn't have to be such a dick about it, though. He'd had an extra two weeks to get his shit together or, you know, talk to her about needing more time. Or, at a minimum, move the freaking jack, so it wasn't a fucking hazard. What right did he have to be pissed off?

She shrugged. "I'm not sure, but you should probably check with the local tow company. Probably on one of their lots."

He scoffed. "Real mature, Leah. Seriously, you couldn't have given me a heads-up?"

She cocked her head. "Oh, I'm sorry. Since you were the one who suggested two weeks in the first place, I thought it'd be enough. Especially when you had double that time and never said you needed more. So..." she trailed off and shrugged. "Maybe if you wanted more than twice the time you originally gave me for helping each other out, you should've said something."

He drew in a deep breath, eyes snapping with his anger. "You know what? Fine. Play it that way."

"I don't know what you're talking about."

He snorted. "Sure. Good luck with that grass, and," he nodded toward where the door hid the bat, "maybe invest in something other than an old bat for protection."

She leaned the bat against the wall and crossed her arms, scowling at him. "Are you threatening me?"

He gave her the look that comment deserved and walked away. She rolled her eyes before swinging the door shut behind him. Melodramatic ass. She turned to the faux mantel where Sadie's ashes rested until they could be spread on the lake.

Gesturing toward the door, she frowned at the box of ashes. "I know what you would say, but he started it. And, frankly, you telling me to give him some grace when he has not shown the same to me is unfair. Especially when that stupid jack could have killed me. And don't tell me I have some blame there too. If you want to preach grace at me, you should still be here. You're supposed to still be here."

Her breath hitched. Fuck this. She was done crying. Today was a good day. She'd get the ditches cleared. She hadn't driven Sadie's tractor, a Farmall 706, in so long. It would take most of her attention.

The tractor wasn't starting. She had to mow the ditches today, and *the tractor wasn't starting*. It always caught on the first try. Sadie babied it. Started it up regularly, drove it to town for kicks and giggles. Why wasn't it starting?

If she didn't mow the ditches today, Liam was sure to capitalize on the miss and make absolutely sure she received a citation for the overgrown ditches. If the same people were in charge as had been for the past century or so, they weren't going to care that she had just lost Sadie and just inherited the farm.

Leah frowned, shaking her head. She tried to start it for the millionth time. Nothing, again. She tried once more, holding her breath and praying to whatever deity deigned to listen. Nothing. She yelled in wordless frustration.

Why couldn't something about this be easy? She was trying to comply with the notice. She'd dealt with the headache from hell from the fuel fumes – usually only a full-on trial could spark that kind of pain. She'd done what she was supposed to do, so why the ever-loving hell was it not working?

She sat up and shook the steering wheel, fortunately moving her body more than the wheel. One more time. It was going to work. She'd sweet-talk it. That worked in the movies.

"Darling, you're such a great tractor. You know you want to start for me, don't you? We can go fulfill your purpose, chow down some grass, so the nasty county people don't yell at Mommy." Continuing to speak encouragement, she held the button, hit the starter, and screamed when nothing happened.

"You know what? Fine, be a bitch." She hopped down, sleeve catching on the clutch as she did and throwing her off-balance enough to swing her into the side of the tractor. Of course, she hit it with the same side that had smashed into the box the day before. *Fuck*.

When she caught her breath, she barely restrained herself from kicking it. She'd only hurt herself more. She got to the door of the shop before she spun on her heel, returning to the side of the 706 to pat it on its side and apologize. She'd call Sam. With any luck, he could come out today and fix whatever was wrong with it.

The next morning, Sam Gallow studied her for a few beats, kneeling by the

706. He glanced back to the tractor, then returned his gaze to her. "You towed his car?"

She sighed, covering her eyes with her hand briefly before nodding. Sam looked over to the empty spot where Liam's classic car had been for years while he tinkered with it. Shaking his head, he laughed softly.

When he straightened to lean against the tractor, laughter danced in his eyes. "Did you tell him you were going to tow it?"

She sighed. "No."

When he snorted, she rolled her eyes, fighting a smile.

"Look, I was upset. When he gave me two weeks to figure out what to do about Athena and Hermes, I gave him two weeks to get his shit off the farm. That was four weeks ago. Then, I found out he lied to me about something, and he left a freaking jack sticking out from beneath the car. I tripped over it." She waved her hands around helplessly before shrugging.

His eyes widened. "You okay?"

She nodded, rubbing her side briefly. "Some bruises. I'll be fine."

"So, he got under your skin?"

She cast Sam a droll look but, as usual, couldn't stay upset with him for long. "Yes," she admitted grudgingly, "he got under my skin."

To give credit where credit was due, Sam fought off the laughter for at least half a minute before he gave in and ended up bent over, hands on his knees as he laughed.

When he was finally done, he nodded at her and wiped the tears from his eyes. Turning, he peered under the fuel tank before nodding. When he gestured her over, he was holding one side of a broken wire. She frowned, studying it until she realized it wasn't frayed. It was cut. Her mouth dropped open, and Sam covered his laugh with a cough.

"What is that?" Leah asked, voice significantly steadier than she felt.

When she looked back at Sam, his eyes were dancing with barely suppressed laughter. "The wire to your starter solenoid."

She sighed, knocking her head lightly against the side of the tractor. "I suppose it can't start without the wire to the starter solenoid."

"Not so much," he agreed.

"I got a fine from the county. Alec showed up early this morning to deliver it."

That fact sparked another round of coughing from Sam's direction. Alec hated her. He hadn't always, but things had fallen apart between them ever since... The Incident. She wondered briefly if he'd told Liam about it before pushing the entire affair out of her mind. It was done. It wasn't worth the mental energy.

She rolled her eyes and shook her head. She could hardly blame Sam for finding humor in the whole crazy situation. If she weren't in the middle of this mess, she might have had the same reaction.

"Can you fix it?"

Sam nodded. "I've got what I need in my truck."

"God bless you," she murmured, fervently grateful.

"So, what are you going to do?"

She sighed. She should take the high road. Too much was riding on her pulling in a solid business partner and/or investor. She couldn't be distracted by this juvenile bullshit with Liam.

"Nothing. I'm going to do nothing." *Probably*, she added silently.

His raised eyebrow clearly conveyed his doubt. When she shrugged, he shook his head, eyes dancing with mirth.

"Fine, don't tell me. Let me know if you decide you'd like a hand."

Chapter Six: The First Test

Leah laughed once more at the photo Liam had sent before forwarding it to Cassidy. Sadie had left clear instructions that Liam was to be invited to the spreading of her ashes, so Leah had grudgingly saved his number. Even if she didn't actually want contact with him.

> Is that glitter?

> It appears to be.

> APPEARS TO BE??? Girl, you actually did it?!?!

> I feel like I should neither confirm nor deny this vague accusation.

> HOLY SHIT, WOMAN!!

> !!!!!

> *laughing face emoji*

> Wow, he's going to be cleaning that up FOREVER.

Leah's smile widened. She spared a brief thought for how unhinged she must look before shrugging it off. She returned to her conversation with Liam. Cassidy would demand a screenshot as soon as she realized there must have been more following the photo. Best to preempt the demand.

> <Image>

> Are you kidding me with this??

> Wow. Who'd you piss off?

> It's EVERYWHERE.

> Yikes. That's a bummer.

> Really, Leah? Really?

> You know, I hate to give criticism at a time like this...

> Maybe don't, then.

> But, if you were a more pleasant person, maybe someone wouldn't have felt the need to exact revenge via glitter.

> Whoops. Sorry, didn't see that last message right

GLITTER BOMBS & SECOND CHANCES

After sending the screenshot, she bit her lip at Cassidy's most recent message.

> away.

> Are you worried about what he's going to do in response?

> He started it. We have exacted revenge. He should just let it go.

> Glitter is a bit of an escalation.

> Feels proportional to me.

> IT'S GLITTER.

> Glitter is the devil.

> He sabotaged my tractor.

> Trespassing and destruction of property.

> Literal, actual crimes.

> Okay, point.

> Is revenge by glitter a crime?

> Feels like it should be a crime.

> I don't think so?

Leah sighed, staring down at her phone. And that was the main problem. The reason she wasn't going to do anything after the tractor. The reason she should have taken the high road. What was Liam going to do next?

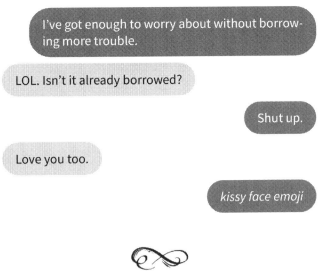

The blaring screech of a car horn shattered her momentary zen. *Damn it.* She had been up half the night, thoughts bouncing between elation that Sadie's dream was closer than ever to coming true and crushing dread that everything was going to come crashing down around her ears.

Her brain had helpfully provided a myriad of ways everything could go wrong. She would then force her anxious lizard brain to picture things going right per her therapist's recommendation. It hadn't helped.

The afternoon before, she'd spun around in the sunlight that filled Sadie's living room with warmth. Rosalee had come through with her connections. Leah would be hosting a small luncheon tomorrow, catered by Rosalee's Diner. Rosalee had introduced her to a variety of potential partners, running the gamut from silent investors to full-on business partners. She'd also be hosting a few owners interested in leasing their horses or leading trail rides. With Sadie's land backing up to a state forest, it was a significant draw.

Sadie would have been so happy to see this come through. She'd wanted to see the little farm come alive again. Now, Leah just had to bring it home, really sell the pitch.

She had finished pushing the boxes into a semblance of order in the barn. The space needed more work, but the potential was clear. The boxes were an easy fix, if she could get the money or labor needed to make the myriad of minor repairs to the barn, fix or replace the fencing, and clear out the trails.

By the time late morning rolled around, she had herself mostly convinced it would work out. The blaring horn did not feel like a good omen. She frowned deeply at the sight of Frank O'Neal's old truck pulling up to the house. She waved away the cloud of dust trying to force its way into her lungs.

What now? She'd just finished setting up for the luncheon. People were going to be arriving any minute. Why would Frank be out now? She closed her eyes as realization hit. Liam. Why hadn't she just let it go? And how bad was this going to be?

Frank's two border collies jumped out of the bed of his truck, shooting off into the pasture to harass the horses. Little terrors. She shouted after them to stop, but, as always, they ignored her. Sadie had warned Frank before that those horses could kill his dogs. Despite the repeated warnings, he brought them out whenever he wanted to sell Sadie on his latest scheme.

Getting out of the truck, Frank shot her his typical cocky grin. The man thought he was God's gift to women. He looked good, and he knew it. Too bad he didn't have the personality to match.

He nodded toward the tables. "Cute spread you got there, Lee."

She ground her teeth at the patronizing tone. The man couldn't be bothered to train his dogs, or give the working breed collies *a job*, but he felt free to dispense judgment everywhere he went. She took a deep breath and pasted on a smile. He wasn't going to get her down. Today was going to be a good day.

"Thanks, Frank. What brings you out?"

"Just dropping off the dogs," he said with a smarmy grin.

Panic dug its icy claws into her.

"I was out with Liam and Alec last night. Liam mentioned you were looking to start up a horse boarding business with maybe some dog sitting on the side. Mentioned you had a big meeting today, and you could use some support, something to show these people you can do what you're saying you can do."

Oh, hell no. She was not set up to dog sit, much less to ride herd on those two hellions. She started to explain the same, but, of course, he spoke over her.

"Sure do appreciate it, Lee," he said loudly, opening the door to his truck and climbing back in. "I'll see you day after tomorrow." He winked before peeling out. When she shouted after him, he simply waved out the window.

Those *assholes*. Him and Liam both. Frank *knew* she'd say no. He was lazy, not stupid. He would've known damn well that Liam was feeding him an excuse to wreak some havoc. While Alec wouldn't have stepped in to help her, it also wouldn't have been his idea. He made no bones about his distaste for being in Leah's general vicinity, but they left each other alone.

What was Liam *thinking*? Whatever inconvenience she had caused him, it was nothing in comparison to trying to wreck a meeting that could save Sadie's farm.

She yelled wordlessly before stomping off to the barn to grab two lead ropes. The damn dogs wouldn't listen to her. She'd have to catch them. She would stash them in one of the stalls. The cats would just have to stay away from that one stall.

It took her an hour, and several words of power that her former mechanic girlfriend taught her, before she managed to catch and stash both dogs. Glancing at the time, she cursed. She'd been well ahead of schedule, and now she needed to clean up all over again. She was a sweaty mess.

Leah watched the flames dancing under the chafing dishes suspiciously. She did not have a great feeling about open flames. The feeling was not helped by the banquet table's position right in front of the old farmhouse. When the first SUV pulled up, she shook her head. Her anxiety was just screwing with her.

Conner Jameson, the too-attractive-for-his-own-good trainer, was considering a move out of the busy barn where he currently worked. She wiped her hands on her pants and walked over to greet him. His brilliant grin was dazzling against his dark skin, and she immediately understood why so many of his students were obsessed with him.

They had barely exchanged pleasantries before Ros, then the remaining invitees arrived. Ros ushered everyone to enjoy the food before returning to Leah's side, making introductions to a few of the more likely candidates for either boarding or renting the space to train students. With Ros's help, she was able to start pitching on an individual level before she gave everyone the tour.

Leah felt a buzz of warmth with how well this was going. Ros had, of course, been right about the individual pitches. It was so much easier to tailor her ideas to each person rather than try to hit on every potential avenue in a larger presentation. Enough people seemed interested that this could really work. The real test would be showing them the barn, outlining exactly what she was looking for from those who were interested in investing, and painting a picture of what the trails would look like once cleared.

She shared a quick smile with Ros before the sound of a cat yowling sent a shiver down her spine. She closed her eyes, dread suffusing her body when the yowling was quickly followed by barking. She slowly turned toward the noise.

Frank's dogs were hot on the heels of one of the barn cats. When she realized it was Screecher, a quiet portion of her brain absently noted the cat was living up to its name. Grayson, snarling, managed to cut off one dog's progress, but the other slipped past.

Screecher made a beeline for the banquet table. He nimbly slipped under one end of the cloth-covered table and out the other. Leah watched in disbelief as the dog followed, collar catching on the tablecloth and jerking it violently forward before dropping free. The dog came out the other end, sniffing around before shooting off in the same direction Screecher took. Eyes locked on the dancing flames as horror replaced her disbelief. The three heaters rattled before tipping over as if moving in slow motion. Flames shot across the tablecloth, quickly engulfing the table.

Numbly, Leah jerked forward, knocking over her chair before grabbing the nearest pitcher to throw on the table. Others followed her lead, dumping the pitchers and glasses of water out on the table, side of the house, and grass until it was sopping wet. Leah stared in silent shock. Her eyes caught on the scorch marks up the side of the historic farmhouse. She blinked rapidly. The house could've gone up too, if it hadn't just rained.

She jumped when someone gripped her shoulder. Rosalee. "I'm so sorry," Leah blurted.

"Oh, honey," Rosalee murmured, "it could happen to anyone. We're going to clear out, give you some space."

Stomach churning, Leah nodded. She turned to the crowd with a weak smile. "Thank you all so much for coming. And," she gestured helplessly at the soaked table, "helping me put this out. I, uh, hope we might still be able to work together."

She managed to hold herself together through the murmured vague assurances, platitudes, and farewells.

After everyone cleared out, Leah tracked down the collies and coaxed them into her car. Closing the door behind them, the car window reflected her scowl and dark eyes. She had a delivery to make.

Chapter Seven: The Fallout

Leah jolted awake, fumbling for her phone to make that *awful* noise *stop*. She stared blearily at her phone screen. Not her alarm. Although, it was past time to get up. Why was she so exhausted?

Her mouth dropped open when the events of yesterday and the evening before flashed before her eyes in technicolor. She didn't actually... Shit. She really hoped that was just a dream. She was not that irresponsible. She was an *adult*. An adult who absolutely did *not* allow her high school sweetheart to make her regress back to the folly of juvenile antics.

"Hey, Lee. Have you, uh... Have you checked your page at all today?" Cassidy clearly figured out she had answered, despite her silence.

Leah blinked, struggling to bring her brain back online to fully process the question. "No. I haven't even gotten up yet. Why?"

Cassidy sighed but was otherwise quiet. A very loud quiet.

"Cass," Leah said slowly, "what is it?"

"So, you know how I'm still friends with Alec online?"

"Yeah," Leah agreed slowly. Alec had only gone scorched earth where his relationship with her was concerned. Cassidy remaining somewhat distant acquaintances with him was to be expected. Where was this going?

"Yeah, so..." When Cassidy trailed off, Leah could practically see her chewing on her lip.

"The buildup is killing me. Cassidy, just spit it out, please."

"Liam posted a rant about you and the farm and," she paused. "Well, a lot of things, really. People being people, they responded."

Leah cursed before flopping back onto her pillows. She covered her eyes with a hand. This was not going to end well.

"Yeah. So, it kind of blew up, and I caught a video or two with some screenshots. They've already been taken down somehow. But, anyway..."

"Did you take screenshots?"

Beyond a sigh, Cassidy was silent on the other end.

"Okay. That's fine. Don't answer that just yet. Tell me what you saw."

"Well, he... he certainly didn't pull any punches. And before you freak out about this hurting the whole *save the farm* plan, I don't think this hurt that. Maybe the opposite, actually. Apparently, he'd gained some pretty good traction in a couple social media realms while building up his journalism credibility, you know?"

Leah sat up, switched the call to speaker and dropped the phone back to the bed. Hands free, she used both to rub her temples. Maybe she could stave off the budding headache.

"It's fine, though. I want to make sure you understand that. I think it actually got some more people interested in what you've got in mind for the place, which is really great for the whole *flee your gross job to find some peace in the country* plan."

"Uh-huh," Leah agreed slowly.

"Right, so back to the gist of it. The majority is definitely on your side. The consensus seems to be that he needs to give you a little grace, especially after everything Sadie did for him. Some people seemed to think he wanted Sadie's farm to be sold off to some developer, and they were hella pissed about that."

Leah groaned. Where did that rumor come from? Please don't let there be some grubby developer out there wanting to turn Sadie's haven into some corporate nightmare.

Okay. It was probably nothing. She needed to focus. "Cass, babe, please just tell me what he said."

"Basically, you should go back to putting your fancy law degree to good use, you're clearly not cut out for country living if you can't even control two dogs, and someone would have to be crazy to trust a city person to know her ass from her elbow in the horse business."

Leah's eyebrows rose as she listened to Cassidy's summary. She couldn't think of a single thing to say.

"He made some vague references to having dated you in the past and narrowly escaping the absolute disaster continuing that relationship would have been, since you're clearly meant for the city."

That was just insulting. Plenty of lovely people were meant for city living, Madison, paralegal extraordinaire and Leah's favorite person at the firm, among them. Leah, however, was not one of them. If it hadn't been for the frequent visits to Sadie's, she'd have suffocated in the city years ago. She rolled her eyes and tuned back into Cassidy's words.

"Basically, a lot of digs about you getting into this business is a terrible idea and not being cut out for the hard work. And, Leah, before you start spiraling down into self-doubt..."

Leah cut her off with a quipped, "Too late." He was right about the horse business. Sadie knew everything. Her lack of knowledge was the reason she needed someone who did know the business in addition to someone who could help with the financing. Preferably, they would be the same person.

"Ah, hell, Lee. Look, he doesn't know what he's talking about. Sure, you don't know much about horses, but it's not like you're proposing you train horses or handle riding lessons. You are making land and trails available and looking for partners who could handle the more technical aspects. If you go into boarding, I know damn well you can brush off your rusty skills for the day-to-day care."

"Right," Leah offered, voice faint. Cassidy was probably right. Ros had sent her a text after last night's fiasco assuring her they were nowhere near the bottom of the barrel with potential prospects. This could still work out.

"And," Cassidy added, "you wouldn't agree to watch dogs like Frank's anyway. You'd do the classes for canine management or whatever and do temperament testing and all that jazz before agreeing to board anyone's dogs. And let's not forget you didn't agree to board his dogs in the first place.

"Sweetie, you're careful and resourceful, and you will absolutely kill it at whatever you put your mind to."

Cassidy was silent for a long moment. "Are you okay?"

"Yes," Leah said firmly before sighing. "No. Yes. I'm fine. It will be fine. Everything is going to be fine."

"Yeah, everything is on fire, but it's fine. Totally fine."

Leah laughed. "One hundred percent fine. It's like you know me or something."

"If it makes you feel any better, I don't think he actually meant to post this. It just doesn't look very polished. Don't get me wrong, I don't like the boy, but he can usually write. It's too rambling. Like he wrote it while he was drunk, or something. But I thought he didn't drink."

Leah sighed. "I wouldn't have thought he'd be inclined, but who knows what's going on inside his head these days? How bad are the comments?"

"Well, the post is already down, and it's shockingly hard to track down screenshots given the age of the Internet. But they weren't great for him.

Couple people are demanding he be fired because someone with that little self-control 'shouldn't be educating young minds.'"

"Doesn't he work at the college?"

Cassidy laughed. "They're still practically babies, and you know it."

Leah snorted. "True, but still."

"Yeah, but still. That was actually a response here and there. A few someones made some noise about him being up for tenure though and having connections on the tenure committee."

"Shit. I. Do not know how I feel about that," she said haltingly. She rubbed her temples again before scrubbing her hands over her face. "Was what he wrote really that bad?"

"It's not good, but the ire is probably overblown for what it is. You know small towns. Frankly, it kinda looks like he wrote an angry diary entry that his sister decided to share with the class.

"Focus on taking your next step forward, ignore the asshole, and use this as fuel for moving forward. Because, girl, you have got this one hundred percent."

"You really think so?" Leah asked, hope kindling without her permission.

"I know so," Cassidy said, voice firm with conviction. "If this surprises you, what I am saying hasn't fully sunk in. Listen, my suggestion, and you can do with it what you will, is to focus your energy on the next meeting. Don't give Liam another moment of your time."

"Thanks, Cass," Leah murmured.

"And maybe no more glitter bombs?"

Leah snorted. "No more glitter bombs."

"Good girl. Now, do not forget that while I know you have totally got this, it's okay to need some help. Let me know if you need anything, okay?"

Leah sighed. She hated needing help. Asking for it was even worse. "Will do."

Cassidy scoffed on the other end of the line. "Liar. Love you. Talk to you later."

"Love you back. Thank you. For the heads-up and... everything else."

"Sure thing, lady."

After they hung up, Leah flopped backwards in the bed. After grabbing an extra pillow from her side, she pulled it over her face and screamed. Pushing the pillow off her face, she groaned when she realized she had forgotten to ask about the screenshots. The little shit had successfully distracted her.

Later that day, shock coursed through her at the sight of Liam's silver car pulling up the drive. Grayson's gaze was fixed on the vehicle, tracking its progress closer to Leah. What the hell was Liam doing here? The *audacity* of the man. To post that bullshit and then pop up here as if he were somehow welcome *the same day as said bullshit.*

After some badgering, Cassidy had relented enough to send her some quotes. When she finished reading, she'd gone out to the barn to work through her mixed emotions. Sorting out the contents of the boxes, so the cousins could decide what to keep and what to donate, had been a no-go. She couldn't concentrate. Instead, she'd decided to work off her irritation in the pasture Hermes and Athena would share for a few more weeks.

The physical labor had started to work until he showed up, striding toward her like he didn't have a care in the world. Deliberately relaxing her jaw, she drew in a deep breath. She would not say anything unfortunate. She leaned on her pitchfork, hoping to fake some level of calm until she actually felt it.

His long legs were eating up the distance too quickly. He'd be on the other side of the fence much too soon. Deep breaths. Those were supposed to help. And, here he was.

"What the hell are you doing here, Liam? Seriously, what the fuck?" Deep breathing was not the answer, apparently. Maybe she needed more practice.

He winced, casting her a chagrined look that appeared a shade too practiced. He was trying to *manage* her. "I take it you saw it, then."

Leah resisted the strong urge to throw the pitchfork at him. She was a reasonable adult, and reasonable adults did not throw things at people. Even if said person was an absolute ass. Later, she'd be appalled she even had the thought. For now, all of her focus was geared toward restraint.

"Yeah, I saw it," she agreed tersely.

"That was never supposed to be posted. I—" He shook his head, cutting himself off.

She scowled when she caught him searching her face for a reaction. He was absolutely attempting to manage her. The only question was why. He didn't need anything from her beyond a cessation of hostilities. She was done. He knew her well enough to know she would drop it at this point.

"I was angry when I wrote it. I never meant for anyone to actually see it."

"Hold up," she said, disbelief clear in her tone. "Is that supposed to make it all better?"

He flinched. She couldn't tell if it was intentional. He'd learned early how to play people, keep the peace. Either his tells had changed, or her anger had actually impacted him.

A muscle in his jaw ticked. He'd noticed her perusal, then. Good. Maybe he'd drop the act.

"You're right, and I am sorry for writing it, but you can't pretend you've never done anything you regret."

"Are you fucking kidding me?" She wanted the act back. He was swinging this back on her? "Are you seriously trying to say the shit you pulled was anywhere near literally anything I've done? Even ignoring that bullshit post, not to mention the *comments*. Jesus." She pushed a hand through her hair.

"Frank's goddamn dogs—thanks *so much* for that, by the way—could cost me this farm."

Her fist tightened painfully around the pitchfork when he rolled his eyes. Full-on rolled his eyes as if she were being dramatic. He almost burned the house down. A house *that had been standing for over one hundred years.*

"Look, let's not get dramatic here, and stop trying to act like you're entirely blameless. We both know that's not the case. Locking Frank's dogs in my office could have cost me my job. They destroyed the door getting out, by the way. Not to mention the rest of the damage."

She sputtered. "Dramatic? Are you... are you kidding me with this? You actively intended to sabotage a meeting that you were well aware was important to me, not to mention this farm. And beyond that—" she waved toward the old house, absently noting her voice was much higher than normal, "—you almost burned the fucking house down!"

He took a step back at her yelling, mouth dropping open. He squinted in the direction of the farmhouse, frowning as he started at it. "It looks fine. What are you talking about?"

She narrowed her eyes. "The dogs chased a cat under the buffet table, which tipped the flames over and lit the entire thing on fucking fire. If you don't believe me, Mr. Fact Checker Man, go ahead and look at the scorch marks. They're still there."

She facepalmed internally. Mr. Fact Checker Man? Seriously? That was the best her brain could give her?

Her mouth dropped open when he looked like he was actually considering walking over there to check her story. Snapping her mouth closed, she reminded herself to take deep breaths. Count to ten. Calm down.

Something. Okay, counting to ten.

He broke her concentration at five. "I had no idea. I'm sorry. That was definitely not my intention."

"Ah, yes," she bit out, "so much better that your intention was only to scare off the investors." She cocked her head, studying him. Cassidy had mentioned a developer. It seemed unlikely, but maybe Liam was working with them.

"Do you actually want some developer to try to turn this into a resort?"

"What?" He sounded genuinely shocked. "No. Why would I want that?"

She dropped the pitchfork when she spread her hands out wide. "Beats the hell out of me, Liam. Why'd you disable the tractor?"

"You *towed* my car."

"You *lied to me* about the rescue situation." At his surprised look, she cast him a tight grin. "Yeah, I found out about that. Ros told me you took Sadie to check out the rescue."

"That—" he started.

She cut him off. "I swear to God, if you tell me it doesn't count because it was a lie by omission, I will scream."

"Okay, yes. Fine. I should have told you. But..." He cut himself off, clicking his mouth shut.

"But?"

"Nothing," he said with a weak smile. "But nothing. I should have told you about the rescue."

She narrowed her eyes, suspicion rising quickly. "Why are you agreeing?"

He frowned. "Why are you so suspicious?"

"Because I know you, maybe?"

He scoffed. "You don't know me. Before Sadie's... Before Sadie, we barely exchanged two words in over ten years."

She crossed her arms. She wasn't doing this with him. "Fine, Liam. I know absolutely nothing about you."

A muscle in his jaw ticked, but he didn't continue the argument. Yeah, he was definitely up to something.

He took a deep breath. "Look, I am sorry about the thing with the dogs, and the county, and the tractor."

He stopped, clearly waiting for something. When it clicked, her barely banked anger rekindled. "Are you looking for an apology from me? Is *that* what you're doing here? Are you kidding?"

"You could have cost me my job. They destroyed my office door getting out. Tore through whatever they could get their grubby mouths around. Hundreds of dollars of damage, minimum."

"What does that have to do with me, Liam? They took off chasing a cat. About a dozen people will back me up on that. If you want to talk about damage, let's return to the point where they almost burned down *my house*. And there's no denying you are responsible for them being here."

"You know what? Fine," he agreed tersely. "We'll go with that for now. I'm *still* finding glitter."

"You cut a wire to make sure I would get a fine from the county. Glitter is a proportional response. Sending Frank's dogs to interfere with a very important meeting is an absolutely out-of-pocket escalation. You knowingly interfered with what I'm trying to do with this farm. And then the cherry on top of that was your post, also attempting to trash my chances with this farm."

"Okay, fine. You have a point. Just," he looked away briefly, "where did the goats come from?"

She couldn't help it. He looked legitimately confused. The scene from the night before played in front of her eyes, and she burst out into laughter. Four teens smuggling two squirming goats into the building had been a sight to behold. She'd barely been able to make out the large numbers written on the handkerchiefs around their necks. One handkerchief sported a large "1"; the second had a "3." Unless they'd already dropped off number two, someone was going to be searching the college campus for a ghost goat.

She braced herself on the fence, bending over with the force of her laughter. When she straightened, he was staring at her, baffled. She wiped away tears from the corners of her eyes and shook her head.

"I didn't have anything to do with any goats. No idea where they came from."

He narrowed his eyes. "You didn't leave them there."

She shook her head slowly. "Nope," she made sure to pop the P. "I didn't leave them there."

"But you saw who did."

She shrugged. "I'm not sure how I could have seen anyone at the college when I was here all night."

"If you didn't see anything, what was the laughter all about?"

She shrugged, mirth still bubbling inside her. "Goats in the college sounds hysterical. I have an active imagination."

This time, his rolled eyes didn't bother her nearly as much.

"Alright, fine. I am sorry about the dogs. I was ticked about the car, and I lashed out. I shouldn't have screwed with your meeting."

She recrossed her arms. "Is this the part where you tell me what you want?"

When he didn't answer, she continued, "Because you do want something, right? You didn't come out here to apologize for siccing the county on me, disabling the tractor so I couldn't actually mow the ditches in time, the dogs, or the cherry on the fucking sundae of spreading exactly what you thought of my quote unquote failures thus far all over social media."

He fidgeted but didn't interrupt her.

"Is that about right?" Her anger drained away, leaving her with plain exhaustion. She didn't have the time or energy to be arguing with him.

"No," she said, voice firm. "I don't want to hear it. Go away."

Spreading his hands, he hesitated before finally blurting, "Look, just let me get this out, please. If you tell me to go away again after I finish, I'll go away. Never to darken your doorstep again."

"Fine," she bit out, waving her hand at him, "proceed."

"I'm up for tenure this year, and some of the committee saw the post. For the members who didn't see it, there were at least three people in the thread who would be happy to rehash it for them in all of its gory detail. My department head is hinting that it's not just tenure that's in question. I need you to help me walk this back.

"If you show you're willing to forgive me, as the injured party, the rest will fall in line. If we make a few appearances together, it'll go a long way toward putting out the fire. I'll pay you for it, of course, and I'll help you grow the boarding business or whatever you want to do with the farm."

Leah studied him silently after he finished, mentally discarding several insults and various forms of "what the fuck" before shaking her head. "No. Now go away."

When he looked like he was about to speak, she shook her head again. "Nope. I heard you out. You have my answer, and now you're going to leave me the hell alone."

"Okay," he said slowly, "I understand you're mad, but there's just one more thing you need to know."

"What," she said, voice flat.

"I managed to talk the department head into holding off on reporting you for trespassing and damage to property. He's agreed to let it go and convinced the board to let it go, if I pay for the damages. I can only afford to do that if I have tenure."

Her eyebrows shot up, and her mouth dropped open. He was actually trying to blackmail her. Holy shit. They couldn't actually prove it was her, but the investigation could certainly screw up her plans. She squeezed the bridge of her nose. Clearly, she wasn't dodging a headache today.

He shot her a grin and took a step back, apparently sensing he'd made all the progress he would today. "Right, I'm just going to give you some time to think it over."

She wanted so badly to smack him. She wasn't a violent person, dammit. "Fine. Just go away."

"'Course." He backed away, spreading his arms to show he was harmless and doing as requested. "Going now."

When he tipped an imaginary hat at her, she almost revised her opinion about reasonable adults, pitchforks, and her capacity for violence.

Chapter Eight: Unto the Breach

> Junior is your best option given the money situation. Make him grovel.

Glancing one last time at Cassidy's message, Leah steeled her spine and knocked sharply on Liam's door. He let her into the apartment with an easy gesture.

"You're going to need to apologize in public. Frankly, that's the only way this is going to be anywhere near believable."

He filled two glasses with water, sliding one her way before leaning against the counter. "You want a public apology, and you think that's going to fix my reputation? What, do you want me to get on my knees and beg for your forgiveness?"

She cocked her head to the side, flicking her eyes up and down his body before grinning slyly. "You always did look so pretty on your knees."

He rolled his eyes theatrically, and she smothered a laugh. She wouldn't admit it, but she'd missed this.

"It doesn't have to be anything quite so grand. We'll go to Rosalee's when it's busy, you'll apologize for being a complete and total ass, and I'll consider forgiving you. It'll be somewhere approaching believable that I would consider forgiving you, if you make the effort."

He cocked an eyebrow, studying her dubiously. "You'd forgive me in exchange for the mild humiliation of a public apology?"

She scoffed. "Oh, hell no. Offer to be at my beck and call for anything I need or want done on the farm for the next, oh, four months. That might just do it."

He snorted. "At your beck and call? This isn't *Pretty Woman*."

"Right, no sex. Unless…" she trailed off suggestively.

His lips quirked before he shook his head, crossing his arms. "No sex."

"Fair enough. If something magically changes, and you'd be up for some casual sex, let me know." She winked and gave him a bright grin.

She enjoyed the blush rising up to his cheekbones more than she probably should have.

He shook his head, dropping his arms back to his side. Bummer. A part of her was hoping to keep it going for a bit.

"Four months of free labor? You really think that's reasonable?"

She shrugged, then took a sip of her water, soothing her dry mouth. "I do. I'll go to the picnic with you, and I'll show up at your work party and one other sighting in or around town."

Narrowing his eyes, he countered, "Three public meetings, work party, and the town picnic. One of those meetings is a dinner with my boss where you will refrain from throwing me under the bus."

"In case you've forgotten, you need me more than I need you. Two public meetings, one of them the meeting with your boss where I will be my charming self," she ignored his scoff, "your work party, and the picnic. Final offer, take it or leave it."

He studied her. Apparently deciding she wasn't bluffing, he nodded. "Fine."

"Great," she said brightly. "Text me some days that work for you to meet at Rosalee's, and I'll see you there. I'll text you a list of what I need help with on the farm."

He sighed. "I'm going to regret this."

She gave him another bright grin and waggled her fingers on her way out the door.

"You can do this. You are a strong, confident, independent woman." Cassidy's soothing tone might have helped more if Leah wasn't already mentally screaming with anxiety.

"Ah, yes. So independent I just got back from asking a man to fix my problems."

"Woman," Cassidy said sharply, "that's not what happened, and you know it."

Leah took a deep breath, releasing it slowly as she parked in front of the cabin. Bouncing her head back against the head rest, she whined, "Life is ridiculous and can slow its fucking roll anytime now."

"You and Liam are both gaining something from this," Cassidy said calmly, voice firm. "*He* is the one who came to *you*. It's not like you went to him begging for assistance. And even if you had, who fucking cares? Needing help from time to time is human nature, and, sweetheart, in case you missed the memo: you are human. You don't have to do everything on your own to be worthy of love or happiness or whatever. I know this may take some time to sink in, so you go ahead and let the shock work through your system."

She laughed softly. "Right. I'm human, and I can do this."

"Yes, you can."

> Tomorrow at 11?

Leah groaned. It was her idea, but it didn't make putting herself at the center of attention any more appealing. At least they'd get it over with soon. Rip off the Band-Aid.

> Yeah, that'd be fine.

> See you then.

She raised her eyebrows, surprised at his atypically short response. She'd expected more of a plan. His words from the day before came back to her. Maybe he had a point. She didn't actually know him anymore. They hadn't been anything beyond ex-partners for more than a decade.

If he didn't want to have a plan going in, she wouldn't request one. She, theoretically, had more control in this situation anyway. If neither of them knew exactly what to expect out of the other, it'd also look more authentic.

She returned her attention to her notes. She wanted to get a head start on the trails. She could have the small forest logged, clearing up some space for the remaining foliage to flourish while getting the existing trails cleared. Unfortunately, the people she trusted to do a good job were booked out into the fall. The mortgage payoff would be due before they'd get halfway through logging.

Sighing, she swapped documents to where she had compiled her ideas for a second attempt at an investors meeting. Rosalee had a second round already lined up, and Conner Jameson had sent her a few leads. Both had loved her idea for a shrimp boil. Ros had made it clear she should focus on clearing out the barn prior to the meeting. It was, after all, the gem of the little farm.

She nodded at her screen decisively, ignoring the dread curdling in her stomach. It was a lot, but she would manage. She would make the final arrangements for the shrimp boil. She'd host it in mid-August, a bit late in the season, but she needed the time. She had to get it right this time.

Satisfied with her prep work, she closed her laptop, mentally running through tomorrow's schedule. The thought of sitting down at Rosalee's with Liam made her nauseous. She toyed with the idea of calling off the whole arrangement. She didn't need his fake apology churning up old resentments.

She leaned her head back and closed her eyes, hoping the throbbing pain would die down before the morning. She would go through with it. The fragile house of cards that was the plan for making the farm succeed couldn't afford having her anxiety run the show.

After grabbing her phone from the couch, she sent a message to Cassidy.

> Meeting him at Ros's tomorrow at 11. I'm freaking out.

> Ah, hell, lady. I'm sorry.

> Anything I can do? Which part is freaking you out?

> Social interaction, lol.

> He's not going to mean it. And I'm just going to have to sit there and act like I believe him??

> Why did I get myself into this? *crying face emoji*

Maybe don't act like you believe him? Frankly, it'd probably be more realistic.

Perfect way to get him to commit to helping you out on the farm (in public) for the rest of the year.

Or, wait, how did you put it? Be at your beck and call a lá Pretty Woman? *winking face emoji*

> Next four months.

> But, yeah, I like it.

> And, yes, haha. At my beck and call.

Should've gone for the rest of the year.

> Ugh, yeah. But.

> My six months with the bank are going to be up at the end of December anyway. If I can't make it work without indentured servitude, then it doesn't actually cash flow.

Ah, indentured servitude. Is that what we're calling his groveling?

> Sounds slightly better in my head than slavery.

> And he's hardly groveling.

> HAHAHAHAHAHAHAHA

> He fucked up. You have presented him a solution to the PROBLEM HE CAUSED ALL BY HIMSELF.

> You are helping him and getting a little benefit out of it too.

> More… payment for services rendered ;-P

Leah burst out laughing. When she calmed down, she wiped the tears from her eyes to see Cassidy had sent another message.

> Feeling better?

> Yes. Blessings upon your house.

> Kisses. Text if you need anything. Anytime, anyplace.

> Love you, boo.

> Love you back.

> You got this, girl.

"Good for you, Leah. Make him sweat it out."

The speaker was an older woman sharing a table with several others Leah recognized. Leah smiled hesitantly, panic growing as she tried and failed to place the woman who apparently knew her.

The woman grinned, laughter dancing in her eyes. "Don't worry, dear, you don't know me. Although it's probably not much of a comfort, you and the tool in the corner are the best gossip in town."

She shrugged when one of her friends shoved her arm lightly. "Oh please, we might as well be honest. Without the work drama, there isn't as much hot gossip to bond over."

She held out her hand as Leah drifted closer. "I'm Clara. Majority vote is definitely on your side."

Leah blushed furiously but clasped Clara's hand.

"Make sure he grovels an appropriate amount, dear. And ignore all of that nonsense about needing to forgive those who have done you wrong. A little grudge here and there is good for the soul. Keeps you young."

Laughing abruptly, Leah thanked her for the advice. "I'll be sure to keep that in mind, Clara. It's good to meet you."

After giving the rest of the group a smile and an awkward wave, Leah made her way to the back booth Liam occupied. At her approach, he slid out and switched sides, leaving her with her back against the wall but facing their audience.

Her ribs twinged as she slid into the space. She pressed a hand against her side. Out of the corner of her eyes, she saw a look of concern flash across his face. She ignored the look, choosing to focus on their waitress instead. She'd probably start another argument, if she told him what happened now.

Their waitress, Elena, quickly took and delivered their drink orders. After confirming they would not be ordering food, she made herself scarce. Clearly, she was as aware of the purpose of this meeting as the rest of the diner's inhabitants appeared to be. Leah caught several glances cast their way, some more blatant that others, in the few minutes since she entered.

She drummed her thumb against the table before looking at Liam for the first time since she sat down.

He raised an eyebrow, studying her in turn.

"What? You asked me here," she said defensively.

"I did," he agreed slowly. "You're usually more punctual. Did something happen?"

She shrugged, mentally cursing herself for pulling at her ribs again. She almost wished for the anger she had felt in the pasture. At least then the emotion would stifle the pain signals.

"I guess some things do change, after all. Nothing for you to worry about. I was caught up in a conversation. Didn't pay enough attention to the time."

"Right, okay."

She sighed. She really wished he'd just get on with it. She was beyond tired, already stressed, and she wanted to put some ice on her stupid ribs.

He shifted uncomfortably. "I'm not sure how to do this."

"Apologize?" she asked, voice snapping with her irritation. "Yeah, I can see how that would be a difficult task for you. You haven't had much practice. Not, of course, for lack of opportunity."

"I suppose I deserve that."

"You suppose you deserve that? Wow." She leaned her forehead against her hands, elbows propped on the table. She refused to flinch when the movement irritated her ribs again.

She sighed. They weren't getting anywhere at this rate. She straightened against the booth. "Starting with I'm sorry is usually the way to go."

When he nodded, a chunk of hair fell in front of his eye. "I am. Sorry, that is."

She snorted. He was sorry his job was in jeopardy.

"You don't believe me; I get it. But I am sorry. I'm sorry that I didn't tell you about the rescue. I could have alleviated some of the stress you and your cousins were under after Sadie..." he trailed off and waved his hand.

That she understood. She didn't want to voice it either.

He took a breath before continuing, "I'm sorry I didn't talk to you about the car and getting it out of there. I had some things come up, and I should have honored that commitment."

Huh. She had not expected this. "I'm sorry I had it towed."

His eyes widened at her interruption. Apparently, they were both surprising the other today.

She shrugged, uncomfortable and almost wishing she could take it back. "I was going to talk to you about it. And then I tripped over the jack handle while moving some boxes." She waved a hand around vaguely. "So, yeah, I let my irritation take over."

His mouth dropped open. "I am so sorry. I forgot all about the jack. Are you okay?"

She blinked, surprised at his reaction. "Yeah. Just some bruises."

He nodded to her side. "Your ribs?"

She bit her lip. "Yeah."

His eyebrows rose. "And?"

She sighed. She hadn't wanted to have this conversation with him. "And the boxes hit my knee. And my arm is a little sore."

"Did you get checked out?"

"I haven't met my deductible. It's not a big deal. Nothing feels broken."

"Leah..." He cut himself off when she narrowed her eyes. He held his hands up. "It's your choice, clearly. But seeing how this is pretty much my fault, will you please get it checked out? I'll cover whatever the charges are."

"You're going to cover a medical bill that could top a thousand, but you thought it might be a struggle to pay for the damages caused by Frank's dogs?"

He flushed.

Watching him squirm was *fun*. He couldn't push back without someone overhearing the less-than-genuine circumstances that led them both here.

"Yes," he said simply. "The medical charges are on me. I didn't put Frank's dogs in my office."

She laughed softly. Of course. "Thanks. I'll keep that in mind. But you were in the middle of something."

She maybe took a little too much delight in his deepening flush, but she figured she deserved it.

"Right. Where was I?"

"I think you were just getting to the point where you decided cutting the wire to my starter solenoid was a good idea."

He clicked his tongue against his teeth. "I overreacted to you towing my car. Disabling the tractor so you couldn't meet the county's deadline was juvenile." His voice was stiff, a little rehearsed, and he was staring at the table in front of her.

She pulled her lips into her mouth, biting down to stifle her laughter. He didn't believe a single word out of his mouth right there. Fair enough. She wasn't about to apologize for the glitter, and she absolutely was not going to admit to smuggling Frank's dogs into his office.

When he looked up, his lips quirked. They were both on the same page here, at least.

"I am *really* sorry about screwing with your meeting by convincing Frank he should drop his little terrors off with you right before the shindig. And I cannot begin to excuse the post. It never should have happened."

She cocked an eyebrow. She expected some sort of justification for the post. Anything from "I was drinking" to "well, you were an ass too." "No excuses?"

"No," he said firmly. "I can give you a reason for my actions, but it certainly wouldn't justify them. Will you let me try to make it up to you?"

She smothered her desire to probe for the reasons. It wasn't the time or place. Now that she had more space from the shrieking rage, she had a sinking suspicion his father was at the center of it. The last she knew, the man was in prison again. Not that a jail cell had stopped Mr. Devlin from wreaking havoc in the past.

"How do you propose making it up to me?"

He seemed more settled. He'd always been better with plans of action than dealing with emotion.

"I deleted the post. I've posted an apology, taking back what I said. I can and will help you promote whatever business venture you choose to pursue to try to make up for screwing up your meeting, hopefully get you a little more reach beyond Ros's extensive contacts."

He leaned forward, rubbing the back of his neck. "I can help with whatever you need on the farm. This offer is not a backhanded way of saying I don't think you can handle it."

Ah, yes, she remembered that part of the post. Cass had eventually given in and sent her a few screenshots.

"I know you can handle your own business, but I can ease the load a little. Be a spare pair of hands. Put me to work. I'll be at your beck and call for the next four months. Whatever you need, I'm your guy."

She nodded slowly. "You do realize that is absolutely going to include taking care of the horses, right?"

"I think I can handle that."

"And that's just the beginning."

"As it should be," he agreed. "So, will that earn your forgiveness?"

"Let's see. You've taken down the post and replaced it with an apology, you'll handle whatever marketing I might need, and you'll be at my beck and call for whatever I want the rest of this year?" She ticked each term off on her fingers as she spoke.

He nodded cautiously, not correcting her adjustment to the terms.

She shrugged. "I don't know, but it's a good start."

He narrowed his eyes. "You don't know if almost six months of free labor will be enough to make it up to you?"

"I don't. Kind of depends on your attitude." She widened her eyes with faux innocence. "I'm afraid that's the best I can do."

He shook his head, closing his eyes as he laughed softly. "Fair enough."

She slid out of the booth and stood. "I suppose I'll see you when I figure out what to do with you."

He nodded, looking up at her. "I'll be there."

She breathed a sigh of relief as she walked away. That was done. On to the next project. Walking past the group of retirees, Leah smiled at their miming of clapping and cheering. She winced internally when Clara waved her over. So close to freedom.

"If you need any ideas, dear, don't hesitate to reach out to us. I'm sure our collective minds can think of some very necessary chores that need doing around that farm."

Leah laughed. "I'll keep that in mind, thanks."

"More importantly," Clara said, "my husband would very much like to speak to you about those trails of yours."

"I'm willing to take all of the ideas I can get for the trails." She nodded toward Rosalee with a smile. "Ros has my number, or you and your husband can stop by sometime day after tomorrow. I'll be there all day."

Clara smiled and patted Leah's hand. "We'll likely see you day after tomorrow, then, dear. Byron likes to move full speed ahead when he gets an idea in his head."

Chapter Nine: A Fitting Farewell

Leah fiddled with her necklace as she watched the gentle sway of the boats in the gray water of the marina. The day felt appropriately overcast, painting everything with a shade of gray as a backdrop to spreading Sadie's ashes in her favorite lake.

"Is it safe to assume things are at least somewhat amicable with Liam, since he drove you here?"

Leah smiled, bumping her shoulder against Paige's when the other woman came to stand by her side. "I don't know if I'd go so far as to say amicable but good enough, I suppose."

Nodding back to the marina house, she raised an eyebrow in question. "And you and Garret?"

Paige rolled her eyes and shrugged.

Intriguing. She aimed a teasing grin at Paige. "You know, I bet Garret could rock a string of pearls and a housewife gig."

Paige pursed her lips, her nose wrinkling as she thought it over. "We're not going to talk about it."

"If you agree to help me fend off all the comments and whatever about Liam, I'll drop it."

"Never to be spoken of again?"

"Ha, no. No way you'll be able to adequately fend off the relatives for the rest of our lives. But, I will agree not to speak of it again for a week, and chances are decent that I'll forget about it after that."

Paige nodded slowly as she contemplated the offer. "Alright," she said, sticking out a hand. "Deal."

Paige released her hand and looked back out at the water. "I would've done it anyway."

Leah shrugged lightly, lips quirking up into a half smile. "I know. I would've dropped it anyway."

"I know."

Leah would have liked to enjoy the peace with Paige for a while longer, but her parents and the aunts and uncles soon joined. Carol Carter scowled up at the marina parking lot. Following her gaze, Leah spotted Liam getting out of his car. He'd waited in the car while she'd gone down to the dock, putting off interacting with her family as long as possible.

"What's he doing here?"

"Sadie wanted him here," Leah reminded her mother.

"Well, yes," Carol agreed waspishly. "I remember that. I didn't think the little asshole would actually come."

Carol actively disliked Liam. Although she'd never had a good reason, she made her disapproval of the relationship abundantly clear. When they broke up, Carol had been elated.

Leah's jaw clenched painfully. "He has just as much right to be here as the rest of us. In case you forgot," she added in a hiss, "he was the one who found her and took her to the hospital."

"Fat lot of good that did her," Carol muttered.

Leah's eyes widened. What the hell? Before she could say something to spark the next Carter Family Drama™, Paige intervened.

"Aunt Carol," Paige said soothingly, "what's important is that Sadie wanted him here. You don't have to speak to him."

Liam reached the dock shortly after. Greeted with the arctic front Carol was giving off, he simply nodded. Leah breathed a sigh of relief when the pontoon captain's entrance broke the awkward silence.

"Everyone ready?" he asked quietly.

"We are," Paige answered firmly. "Thank you again for fitting this in so quickly. I'm sorry the news had to interrupt your vacation."

Leah mentally crossed her fingers that Paige's subtle reminder would work. The man was doing them a favor. He did not need to be drawn into the family drama. Sadie's letter had been blunter.

> *Alright, everyone, this lovely gentleman is doing us a huge favor. So, we are going to shove down all of the accrued bullshit and act at least halfway decent around this man. Failure to meet this minimum expectation shall be met with your ejection from the boat. To be clear, I don't care where the boat is located at the time of your ejection. You're all sufficiently capable swimmers. I've extracted promises from undisclosed participants to ensure my instructions are met.*

Smothering her grin at the memory of Sadie's words, Leah followed the captain to his boat. Derek, holding Sadie's urn securely, sat on the bench behind the captain's seat. Cassidy slid next to him, and their parents, Frank and Sandra Sanders, took up the rest of the bench. Paige and her parents, Kara and Aiden Wilde, sat on the bench at the back of the boat.

Leah chose the bench seat immediately opposite Derek. Her parents,

Gideon and Carol Carter, lowered themselves onto the bench next to her. Leah groaned internally when her mother spread out to take up the remaining space on the bench. Her father arched an eyebrow but complied with Carol's silent demand to do the same. Liam smirked at the sight before striding to the front of the pontoon and slinging himself into the seat next to the captain.

No one spoke during the trip out to the center of the lake. The light anchor dropped into the water with a quiet splash after the captain cut the motor. Slowly, everyone stood, looking out over the lake. Water lapped against the edge of the boat, rocking it gently. Sadie would have loved it.

Carol cleared her throat, making Leah flinch at the sudden noise. "Is anyone going to say anything?"

Leah's face flamed when everyone looked to her. Time to say something.

"Right. Sadie left instructions. No speeches, but she wanted a verse read before we spread the ashes. Then, a song while spreading them. She said we should wait until we were ready to spread her ashes before we opened it."

Sandra Sanders raised her eyebrows. "Are you going to read it, then, dear?"

Her face flamed hotter. "Oh, sorry, no. I don't have it."

"Right, that's my cue. Sorry, Lee. Sadie asked that I bring it out and read it, and," Cassidy waggled an old iPod, "the song is cued up on here."

"Not sure which one she chose though. Hey," she added, voice bright, "maybe Sadie is going to Rick Roll us."

She pulled a folded-up sheet of paper out of the envelope. As her eyes skimmed the words, her mouth dropped open. She sucked in her cheeks lightly before clearing her throat.

"Jesus wept," she read. Her voice shook with suppressed laughter.

"Huh," Paige said, voice colored with recollection. "She told me I should use that for my confirmation verse."

Derek laughed so hard, the box of ashes rattled in his grip. Leah clapped a hand over her mouth, smothering her giggles. Sadie had told her the same. Carol's scowl and the half grin on Liam's face competed for her attention in her peripheral vision.

Choosing to ignore both, she looked to Cassidy. A large grin spread across the other woman's voice. "That's so Sadie," she mouthed. Turning back to her brother, she asked if he was ready to proceed.

Nodding, Derek set the box on the boat seat and removed its lid. Picking it up, he angled it over the edge of the boat, prepared to slowly pour the ashes into the wind. "Ready."

As Cassidy hovered her finger over the play button, Derek began slowly dumping out the ashes. When "Another One Bites the Dust" by Queen played over the small speaker, he let out a bark of laughter, jostling the box and dumping the ashes out in a large clump.

A large gust of wind saved Sadie's remains from an ignoble plop into the water. Instead, the ashes danced away from the boat in an unexpected riot of color. Someone had added a rainbow of glitter to the ashes.

Frank Sanders bent over from the force of his whoop of laughter. His unique laugh set off the rest of the family, except Carol. She'd never much cared for Sadie's brand of humor. Eventually, the raucous laughter petered out into the occasional giggle. Liam's eyes crinkled deeply at the corners as his eyes danced with mirth.

Wiping the tears of laughter from her eyes, Paige said, "That was very Sadie. Always trying to make a joke to alleviate the discomfort."

Carol forced a smile. "Yes, definitely something my sister would cook up."

Chapter Ten: Moving Forward

Leah set aside her pyrography pen, taking a last inhale of the smell of burning wood before the exhaust fan took it away. She flexed her hand several times before shutting off the alarm. She'd set it to give herself enough time to get outside before Clara arrived. Sitting back, she focused on her piece. She'd made more progress than she thought she'd be able to make.

She'd been working on a large slab of live edge cherry wood. She'd completed the outline of the dragon in flight spewing flames, colored with different species of wood she'd painstakingly inlaid into the larger piece. She had the bulk of the scene done, but she was still working on the time-consuming scales.

She'd been using the studio space every chance she had, unspeakably grateful for the excuse Ros gave her to focus on it. Tasha, the gallery owner Sadie had introduced her to last year, had expressed interest in showcasing the unfinished piece.

It was coming together beautifully but still needed as much time as she could spare. Leah sighed as she cast her mind over the to-do list. Even with help, the jobs ahead were massive. She could let some of them go and focus on her piece. She bit her lip as she considered. Tasha was beyond excited about the piece she was working on. It could kick off a new career for Leah.

She shook her head. The farm needed to be the priority. She'd have more chances with her art. This was the only chance she'd have to keep Sadie's land. Tasha had already accepted a few of Leah's smaller pieces into the show. Tasha was firm in her belief the pieces would sell, but the farm had to be Leah's priority.

She still needed to find an investor or a partner, preferably a partner with some cash to invest. Ros suggested hosting a shrimp boil. The older woman wanted an excuse to be involved with one since she'd visited her sister last fall. The highlight of the trip had been a shrimp boil at a vineyard.

Leah had reservations about wooing potential investors or partners with food again, but Rosalee's excitement had convinced her. She had, however, put her foot down over the method of cooking. No open flames. Not again. Fortunately for Leah's sanity, Rosalee had relented and agreed to help her source induction cooktops for the event.

The shrimp boil would provide the opportunity. Step two was getting the farm ready to wow. With the extra help, she could take on bigger projects. The trails were the obvious priority. It would take a great deal of effort to get them all clear in time to make a difference for the potential investors, but she could clear at least a couple with Liam's help. Plus, whatever Clara's husband had in mind.

Right—Clara. She needed to go meet them. After jogging down the steps, she strode across the pasture quickly, reaching the fence just as a car pulled up the drive. She waved before giving Grayson a brief scratch below the chin. He'd trotted out to investigate the noise before she'd made it down the steps. Clara and her husband, Byron, popped out of the car spryly.

After the introductions were made, Byron jumped straight into business. "I wanted to talk to you about a potential joint venture with those trails. How do you feel about snowmobiles being out here in the winter?"

He continued before she could decide what she thought about it. She smiled at his clear excitement. She liked him already.

"Now, I know it'd be noisy, so we could definitely limit it to the weekends or something, but my snowmobile club was just looking into ways to expand membership. And this could be really great for that. We'd help clear out the trails, of course, and the camping profits would be entirely yours. I was thinking we'd help you keep it clear in the off-seasons, too, of course, and we'd get out the word. We can work out the details of what exactly membership perks would come with. If it's camping limited to members or what. We don't want to get in the way of you earning money on your place.

"The state land doesn't have much of anything in the way of winter accommodations, but I know Sadie ran water out to the barn throughout the winter, and there's that bathroom, right?"

Leah blinked, attempting to process the onslaught of information. "Uh, yeah. She has water out there, and the barn has a full bathroom."

"Excellent," he said, bouncing forward as he spoke, "so here's what I'm thinking."

Out of the corner of her eye, Leah caught Clara smiling fondly at her husband.

"The state land this place backs up to allows snowmobiles, which is, of course, super popular with the local club. But there aren't many options for out-of-towners to stay overnight, and it's a real pity because those trails are beautiful. It could be a real draw to the town, bring in some of that almighty tourism dollar. You with me so far?"

Not entirely, but she'd catch up eventually. Instead of asking him where he was going with this, she nodded.

Clara's smile grew, likely catching that Leah was, in fact, a little lost.

"Wonderful." He clapped his hands together lightly, grinning as he looked out to the trees surrounding the property.

"Anyways, the club itself could surely use more money, and Clara here told me you have someone in your pocket who could draw some attention to the area. What do you think?"

She thought she still wasn't entirely sure where he was going with this. She'd let them use the trails, of course, and Liam would advertise, but that didn't fix the overnight accommodations problem. If she brought in the horses for income, the barn was out for somewhere to sleep.

The farmhouse was a nonstarter. She couldn't imagine letting strangers in to potentially trash the place, and there wasn't any running water in the old house anyway. She definitely didn't have the funds to add a building to the place to accommodate overnight guests. Since the club was looking for more money, they didn't have the money to add accommodations either.

"Dear, you might want to get into what you were actually thinking about Leah's contributions to your idea."

Leah could have kissed the woman.

"Oh," he exclaimed. "I thought I'd already outlined it."

When he looked at Clara, she shook her head, eyes twinkling. He smiled, eyes crinkling at the corners before tearing his attention away and back to Leah.

"Oh, whoops. I was thinking, if you're okay with it, we can use this huge yard of yours for winter camping. Can't say I entirely understand the appeal myself, but I've been told it's popular and fun. Especially with some of the snowmobile crowd. Our granddaughter sends us adorable videos of families out there breaking the ice off their tents and then crawling out with a baby in tow. Cutest thing."

Leah grinned. That would be adorable to see. She was also relieved to finally be on the same train as Byron. She liked where he was going with this.

"Anyways, does hosting some campers and maybe acting as a sort of staging area sound okay to you? We were thinking there'd be a lot of people interested in accessing the trails this way but not so much the camping. If you'd be okay with it, we could store some trailers and machines out here. Again, I'll make sure you get very reasonable compensation out of this. I know it'll be a hassle on your end. And I've heard about the developer interest in this place. It'd be a real shame to lose this gem to some corporate nightmare."

Clara cleared her throat, catching their attention. "He means, would you be willing to consider it, dear? We're not asking for you to jump on board with the idea right away. He just wants to make sure the idea doesn't want to make you run away screaming before he lays it all out or gets any further with brainstorming with the club."

"Right," Byron agreed with an easy grin. He nodded to Clara. "Don't know what I'd do without her. She keeps me on track."

"The idea sounds really lovely, but you should know there's a pretty heavy mortgage on the land. My ability to refinance is dependent on getting funding or a solid plan for revenue in place by the end of February."

"That's alright, dear," Clara assured with a smile. "Even if we can only implement the idea for a good chunk of the winter, we think it's still worth pursuing."

"Of course," Byron agreed after a nudge from his wife. "And I know the club doesn't have much now, but I really do think this idea could bring in some good revenue for the club and Sadie's place here. Maybe it could help with your refinance."

Leah sighed, relieved they were still interested. "Tell me more."

Byron bounced in place again, eyes dancing as he was given free rein to outline his plan. When he finished outlining his ideas for setting up rough campsites and an area for storing snowmobiles for rent, she took them through the trails. The work that appeared daunting to Leah seemed to absolutely delight Byron. The more obstacles they ran into, the more he lit up.

Before they left, Clara took her aside to tell her Byron had been itching for a big project like this. While Leah didn't foresee this being as large of a moneymaker as Byron seemed to think it could be, she was grateful for the help and the possibility of even a little extra income. The experienced help with the trails alone was worth the potential aggravation of hosting winter campers.

Things were really coming together.

Leah shot up in bed. Someone was at the door. She frantically cast her mind back over the last couple of days. She hadn't had any vehicles towed lately. Who was here so early? Her mouth dropped when she saw the time. She'd been up late the night before, working on her latest piece. The detailed work on the scales was meditative, making it a little too easy to lose track of time.

Stumbling out of bed, she grabbed her too large sweatshirt, pilfered from Dolly, her former college roommate slash friend with *phenomenal* benefits. She pulled it on, then worked her fingers through her hair as she moved toward the cabin's front door.

She blinked up at Liam, thoughts whirring and coming to no conclusions as to why he was standing on the porch. Dirt was smeared across his hands, and a single streak marked his cheekbone. Again, why did he have to be so attractive? Pity *they* couldn't indulge in the benefits she had with Dolly. Double pity that Dolly had gallivanted off out of the country after college.

He was silent as she pulled her thoughts together. "Do you need something?"

"I'm working on the trails," he said slowly, brows furrowing.

She quashed the small spike of guilt that she wasn't already out there helping him. She'd planned to be out there, but he didn't need to know that.

"Yeah, that's great. Thank you for following through on your end of the deal. Why are you at my door?"

"If we're going to get the town to believe that you've actually forgiven me, we're going to need to spend some time together." His tone was way too patronizing for the too little amount of sleep she'd had.

"Liam," she said, matching his tone, "no one is here right now to see whether I'm working with you."

"True for the moment, but it's almost noon, and Byron will be here with his crew any minute."

She groaned. How had she slept so late? "Well, hell, at least the town gossips will believe I'm acting with the appropriate amount of vengeance."

He snorted but didn't otherwise reply, clearly waiting for her to figure out what she was doing.

"I'll be out in a bit. Which trail were you working on?"

"The one you had marked. Goes up past the picnic table."

Her eyes widened. Was he insane?

"Yes," she hissed, "the one I marked to *not* do alone. It's ridiculously overgrown, and I still haven't figured out how many trees are blocking that trail, much less whether any of it's too washed out to be standing on. Byron is bringing people who actually know what they're doing."

Crossing her arms to still their movement, she scowled. "What were you thinking? If something happened, no one would know where to look for you!"

The second his lips tipped up into a smirk, she knew she'd screwed up.

"Aw, Lee. You do care," he crooned.

"Yes, Liam," she bit out, mentally cursing her growing blush. "You caught me. I don't want you to die. If that's what you count as caring, yes, I care."

He grinned. "I'll take what I can get."

"You need therapy," she said flatly. "So much therapy."

She slammed the door in his face, but his laughter carried through it. He was a lunatic. She didn't *care* about him, care about him. She just... She shook her head. Nope, she wasn't having this conversation with herself.

"So," Liam asked, drawing out the word, "are we not going to talk at all?"

Leah blew hair out of her eyes before looking back at Liam. They'd been piling large branches and the logs Liam had cut that morning into the back of Sadie's side-by-side. Because of course he'd been operating a chainsaw without telling anyone.

She shrugged before blowing the stubborn chunk of hair out of her face again. "Is there something in particular you wanted to talk about?"

He shrugged. "Dealer's choice."

"And if dealer's choice is silence?"

He laughed. "That's not a topic. C'mon, Lee. There's gotta be something in that big brain of yours that you want to talk about."

"Maybe I was enjoying the quiet."

At his exaggerated pout, she looked away to hide her grin. Based on the sound of his quiet laughter, she was unsuccessful.

She tossed another log into the bucket of the side-by-side. What was a safe topic with Liam? She didn't need a reminder of how easy it was to talk to him about anything and everything.

"I guess we could go over next steps."

"Seems pretty straightforward to me. Byron and Co. are going to show up later today. We'll make progress on the trails, the snowmobile club will get hyped up to finish quickly, and then on to cleaning out that monstrosity of a barn all in time for your August meeting. And then you'll be on the verge of making Sadie's dreams come true and giving up that career you worked so hard for."

He shrugged at whatever her face was doing. She wasn't quite sure what she was feeling, so it was probably some variation of *what the fuck*? They weren't just Sadie's dreams; they were hers too. And that career was draining the life out of her one contested custody case at a time.

"I think you have your next steps pretty well planned out. Just like always."

"Hold up a minute." She frowned, holding up a hand in the universal gesture of stop. "What is that supposed to mean?"

He dug his shovel deeper into the ground, attempting to uproot the stubborn clump of weeds he'd been attacking. He didn't look at her. "You know what it means."

"Pretty sure I really fucking don't," she shot back.

He finally turned back to her. A muscle in his jaw ticked. "Lee, as long as I've known you, you've had a plan for your life."

"So? What's so bad about a plan?" How had they gotten here? Why couldn't they have just continued working silently?

"Nothing," he sighed, bending down to pull up the freed weeds before tossing them in with the rest of the brush. "There's nothing wrong with having a plan."

And yet, his tone implied the complete opposite. She crossed her arms, scowling. He ignored her, returning to the work. That wasn't going to work for her.

"Nope, you started this. Clearly, you want to go somewhere with it. I'm not doing this passive aggressive bullshit with you."

He rolled his eyes as he straightened to face her again, arms slightly spread. "Who's being passive aggressive? I'm agreeing with you."

She snorted. The hell he was. "Clearly, this is something you wanted to talk about. So tell me. What's wrong with having a plan, Liam?"

He shifted his weight, studying her. "It just doesn't leave a lot of room for…" He trailed off and waved his hand. "Can we just forget it?"

She rubbed her temples. "I don't think we can, no," she said softly. "It doesn't leave much room for what?"

"Nothing. Seriously, I'm just tired or whatever."

She groaned. "Seriously? You were the one who wanted to talk. A plan doesn't leave much room for… what? Flexibility? Change? Other people?"

His jaw clenched. Hit the nail on the head. He couldn't be serious. "Are you fucking kidding me? You broke up with me!"

"You were a year, maybe two from walking away from me. I simply saved us some time. Community college at fucking Clearwater didn't fit into your plan. *I* didn't fit into your plan."

"Yes, I had a plan," she hissed. "I adjusted the plan when it didn't serve me anymore. When it didn't fit the people I wanted it to fit. Are you seriously trying to tell me that you broke up with me because you decided I needed to follow a plan I made as a teenager? Right after you got done saying plans are fucking stupid?"

"Okay, no. I didn't say they were stupid."

She wanted to throttle him. "You sure as hell implied it. What the hell, Liam?"

"You're right. I'm being stupid. I thought I was over it."

"Over what?" she bit out.

"Your plan," he said, waving his hands. "You decided to change it and make me decide between you resenting me and losing you."

Her mouth dropped open. Make him choose? She didn't *make him* do shit. "It wasn't all about you. For fuck's sake. I changed my mind, and I had plenty of time to change it back. And what, instead of talking to me about it like a sane human being, you just broke up with me?"

Before he could answer, honking coming from the front yard startled both of them. Byron and his crew.

She pointed at him. "We're not done."

Chapter Eleven: That Is My Circus

Leah sat back in shock. "Slow down," she said, voice breathy with panic. "What are you talking about?"

She had been called into the bank to discuss Sadie's mortgage with the new senior loan officer, Mark Conner. They were making excellent progress on the trails. It was moving along faster than she could have dreamed. There were more club members interested in tooling around in the woods than she'd expected. Bonus, they knew what they were doing. Everything had been coming together. And now, it was all falling apart.

"I am sorry, Miss Carter. It's bank policy that a mortgage with this debt-to-equity ratio be refinanced within three months of the date of transfer when such transfer is pursuant to a death. We are appreciative of the grieving process, of course, but in order to cover our liabilities, we must have a cutoff point."

"Mr. Smith told me I could have six months to refinance as long as I kept up on the mortgage payments. I've been making the payments."

"You must have misunderstood. Bank policy is three months, not six."

Leah shook her head, "No, I didn't misunderstand. He told me I could have until the end of December to refinance the farm. I don't think you understand the work that needs to be done or the work that's already been done."

"I don't need to understand the work the farm needs, Miss Carter. I need to look out for this bank's best interests. What I do understand is that you are simply not a good bet."

Her heart beat against her chest, echoing in her ears. Panic and anger warred for dominance. How was this happening?

He cast her a patronizing smile. "Why don't you do yourself a favor, Miss Carter, and sell the land yourself? The bank has already heard from a potential developer. From what I've seen, this town could use something fresh."

"Mr. Conner," Leah said tightly, "I understand you're new to Clearwater and may not appreciate how things are typically done around here. This bank has always looked out for its neighbors."

"Yes, well, in case you missed it, bad loans caused a massive crash to this economy. The bank risking its money on a bad bet is not looking out for its neighbors. If that's the unwritten bank policy, it's a good thing I'm here."

"That's astoundingly arrogant. The bank has done perfectly well investing in its community."

He scoffed, arching an eyebrow. "Ms. Carter, I didn't realize you worked for the bank. You should be meeting with someone else, if that is the case."

Her jaw clenched so tight, her teeth hurt. "I don't work for the bank."

"Oh, my mistake. You spoke so confidently about how private banking matters were going. I assumed you must have spoken from a place of knowledge."

Her nails bit into her palms. She took a deep breath. She didn't know what he'd do if she continued antagonizing him. She needed to walk this back.

"Regardless of how you think things have been handled in the past, I am here to follow bank policy as it's written. Not as you feel it should be handled. Preserving this bank's assets is my concern. You have until the end of next month to pay off the mortgage, or the bank will be selling the property."

Leah blinked, mind reeling with the threat. "You can't do that. You can't sell it without foreclosing. And the foreclosure process takes months."

"You will find that the bank can. Your aunt executed an assignment of occupation rights in the event she defaulted on the loan. She defaulted."

Her mouth dropped open at the callous statement. He was seriously trying to call her aunt's death a default. Moments after he just said the bank's policy was three months after death. Besides the status of the supposed default, an assignment of occupation rights didn't exist. At least not as far as she knew. What the hell was he trying to pull here?

With effort, she forced herself to pay attention as he droned on, "The bank required a little extra assurance given the debt-to-equity ratio, and your aunt complied. Now, the bank has the option of utilizing that extra assurance."

"My aunt is dead, Mr. Conner. The assignment of occupation rights, if such a thing even exists, isn't valid. I hold title to the property now, not my aunt. If you wanted this alleged assignment to hold any water, you should've recorded it earlier."

His eyes narrowed. He didn't expect her to push back on the legality of the bank occupying the land prior to foreclosure.

"I suppose you could complain to the Court about it, Miss Carter, but I assure you, you would be wasting your time. Fail to pay the mortgage in full by the end of next month, and the property will be sold to one of the developers we've already heard from. Don't let your emotions get in your way. Sell the property yourself, pay off the loan, and move on with your life."

Leah resisted the almost overwhelming urge to deck the smarmy asshole. "Under this alleged bank policy that is only being brought up now, weeks after Mr. Smith gave me until the end of December, I would have until the end of September to pay off the mortgage, not the end of next month. The title was transferred at the beginning of July. I'm assuming, based upon your emphasis on paying it off rather than refinancing, that the bank isn't interested in assisting me with a refinance?"

Mark smiled tightly. "That's correct. You simply aren't an acceptable risk."

She scoffed. Not an acceptable risk her ass. "The mortgage is barely more than what I make in a couple of years practicing as an attorney." She paused to enjoy his look of shock.

Standing, she bared her teeth at him in a fake smile. "Thanks so much for your time, Mr. Conner."

Spinning sharply on her heel, she strode out of the bank and slid into her car. Her hand shook with her fear and anger as she buckled her belt.

Pulling out of the parking spot quickly, she was well on her way back to Sadie's before her breath started coming in shaky gasps. She managed to hold off her tears until she was in sight of the farmhouse. Pushing the gearshift into park, she climbed out of the car before collapsing on the ground, sobs racking her frame.

She heard the crunch of gravel as someone slid to sit beside her on the ground before she registered Liam calling her name. Spotting his worried expression through her tears, she could only shake her head when he asked what was wrong. When he cupped her shoulder in his broad hand, she crawled into his lap. He immediately wrapped his arms around her, cradling her as her tears soaked into his shirt.

When she calmed down, she had no clue how much time had passed.

"You okay?" His voice was tender.

"Not so much," she said shakily.

"Do you want to tell me what happened?"

Her breath hitched when she took a breath to answer. "The fucking bank is calling Sadie's mortgage due. I have to pay it off by the end of September. Asshole tried to tell me end of August, and he tried to pull some weird shit about occupancy rights. Jesus. I don't even know. But the policy he insisted controlled the situation allows three months from the date of transfer. So, September. Fuck. I thought I had more time to pull the money together."

Liam stiffened. The change, made more obvious by being in his arms, pulled her out of her doom spiral.

"What mortgage? Sadie had the place paid off."

She shook her head, crawling out of his lap to sit beside him with her back against the car. She sighed shakily, resting her head against the door. She rubbed her temples, trying to soothe the pounding ache before she addressed his question.

"She re-mortgaged it. I don't have the exact number, but it's," she waved a hand in the air, "it's too much for the bank to accept a simple refinance without some additional money down, but I'm starting to think that has a lot more to do with the loan officer wanting ownership to change to a developer. He's probably got some sort of deal in place to get an off-the-books kickback or something."

She hit her head lightly against her car as a new thought occurred to her. "Jesus. Who knows what the hell some developer would do with this place?"

"Shit. It's really that bad?"

"Yeah, it's that bad."

"I had no idea," he said, voice soft. "Fuck, and those dogs at the meeting."

She laughed before squeezing the bridge of her nose. "Yeah, I was feeling particularly violent because of that."

He winced, looking out at the land in front of them. "No kidding. I had no idea." He frowned, turning back to her. "Why didn't you say anything? I could've helped."

She shook her head in disbelief. "What? Are you serious? I was supposed to think you'd help me why, exactly?"

"Hey, come on. You know what Sadie meant to me. You have to know I would've done whatever I could to help."

This fucking day. She noted in some distant part of her brain that she probably wouldn't ordinarily be this angry at what he said. Maybe she would've acknowledged the hurt he was clearly feeling and even agreed with him. Instead, she was at the end of her rope, and her frustration won out.

"You know what, fuck you very much. If we're looking beyond the fact that you just wrote that post taking cheap shots at me, so I am completely justified in not looking at you as the white knight to solve all of my problems?"

She paused, catching his wince out of the corner of her eye before she continued, losing steam as she did. "You broke up with me and told me you never wanted anything to do with me again. Kind of a shitty way to break up, by the way. Could've been a little less of a dick. Then, the first time we really talk in years, you tell me to get my shit together and stop relying on your help with the horses."

She slumped back against the car, suddenly feeling defeated. "But, hey, turns out breaking my little teenage heart does not, in fact, hold the title for my worst breakup. That honor goes to the man who cheated on me with my roommate. Congratulations. Clearly, you are one hundred percent trustworthy, and I am crazy not to have thought of you."

"Who cheated on you?" His voice was tight, carefully controlled.

"Nope." She pushed herself up to standing. "I'm not doing this. Thank you for your assistance with my emotional breakdown. I'm going to go figure out how to dig myself out of this latest shit storm."

"Well, this fucking sucks." Cassidy bit her lip, worry clear on her face.

Leah nodded glumly. She'd updated Cassidy, Paige, and Derek over a video call.

"I second that," Derek muttered. "What the hell is the bank doing? Which loan officer?"

"He's new in town; you wouldn't have heard of him. Mark Conner."

"Ohhh," Cassidy drawled. "I have heard of him, actually. Rumor has it he got caught sleeping with his boss's wife in the city, and he was booted to the Clearwater branch as some sort of punishment."

"Dude, no shit?" Derek asked.

"No shit." Cassidy's grin was sly.

Leah was in awe. "How... how do you even hear about things like this? How come *I* didn't hear about this?"

Cassidy laughed. "I'm just that good."

"Fine, don't tell me."

"If it makes you feel any better, I have not figured out why they didn't just fire him." She shrugged. "Best guess is he had something on the boss that was enough to stay employed but not in cush-ville."

"Ah, so your super spy network does have its gaps."

Cassidy stuck her tongue out at her brother. "Not so many gaps that I don't know what you were up to last summer."

"Wait, wait. What was he up to?" Paige looked delighted at this new direction. Leah was grateful for the emotional reprieve.

Derek was shaking his head. "Do not."

"Ooooo, it's gotta be goooood," Paige crowed. "Tell us."

Cassidy's gaze shifted across the screen, while Derek's eyes narrowed further.

When she opened her mouth, Derek pointed at the camera, expression stern. "Panama!"

Cassidy's mouth dropped open. "You little asshole."

"Oh, don't you act like you didn't start it. I am an adult, and whatever I did or did not get up to last summer is none of your business."

Leah shook her head, cutting Paige off. "You don't want to ask. You won't get an actual explanation, and we'll be here forever."

Cassidy and Derek wore identical smug expressions. Leah rolled her eyes at their antics.

"Okay," Paige agreed slowly. "Anyone have any ideas on how we save the farm? You've been outvoted on considering this a 'you' problem, by the way, Lee. We are here to help. Sadie's farm means a lot to us too."

Derek winked. "We've got your back."

"And no getting emotional," Cassidy added sternly.

Leah smiled. "Alright. No getting emotional. Any ideas on how we survive?"

"Yeah, actually," Cassidy said. "What if you start selling tickets to the shrimp boil, invite the investors Ros was talking about to come out for free, see what it looks like with people out, and let people know if there's enough interest, you'll do another?

"Then we're not just banking on an investor or a business partner. It's possible a single event could bring in quite a bit of cash. That plus boarding could be enough potential income to get the financing. Liam could advertise, right? He can draw in some people from farther out. Hype it up a bit to try to get some out-of-town interest. If it works out, you could easily make it an annual event."

"I'm free a couple weekends in August, so I can help out, increase your capacity," Derek said.

"Same here," Paige offered.

Cassidy shrugged. "I'd offer if I could, but you know it's a crazy train over here. I will put together some excellent decorations, though."

"That is a great idea, thank you. I'll text Liam about putting together a plan for advertising the shrimp boil, and I'll talk to Ros about what she thinks. We might need a food license or something. She'll know."

"Thank you all. Seriously. I was freaking out."

"It's what we're here for, Lee," Derek said. "We'll all keep thinking of something else you can do on the farm. Any progress on cleaning out the barn?"

"Yeah, it's going pretty well, actually." She paused and tilted her head to the side, picturing the barn before she winced. She had made a lot of progress the night she ran into Liam's car, but it was still packed in there.

"Okay, a lot of progress has been made, but it was an absolute mess. And we're pretty stalled out since we started focusing on the trails again."

She sighed, rubbing her temples. "I should refocus on the stalls, for sure. Some of the relatives have trickled out to remove their stuff, but the stalls could use another cleaning. Clearing out the rest of the arena is going to be a lot of work, to say the least."

Chapter Twelve: The Picnic

She finished shimmying into her favorite yellow sundress as she heard Liam's knock. Snagging her black lace shrug off the back of the couch, she pulled it on as she walked to the door. Liam leaned against the porch post wearing dark jeans and a black button-down with the sleeves rolled up past his elbows. It was a good look on most men, but *damn* could he pull it off.

She paused to admire the view and noticed him returning the favor. He shot her an appreciative grin and wink. Say what she would about his faults, the man knew how to acknowledge effort without being a creeper.

"Ready?" he asked.

"As I'll ever be."

When he turned and offered his bent elbow, she slipped her hand through. The memories came back too easily. It was a mirror image of prom. Of course, they'd both been wearing fancier clothing then. She'd found a red dress that hugged her curves in all the right places. He'd splurged and rented a tux. The thought of seeing him in a tux as an adult sent a surge of longing through her that she ruthlessly suppressed. She was not going to fall for him again. She refused.

After he shut her door, she watched him walk around the front of the car and slide into the driver's seat. He tapped his thumb on the steering wheel twice before shaking his head and starting the car.

Preferring to avoid conversation, Leah looked out the window. The grass was encroaching onto the gravel drive, narrowing the already small path. She sighed mentally. One more project to add to the ever-growing list. She'd already had to take a step back from the art. She continued to hold up her agreement with Ros, but she wasn't getting lost in it. No more wondering where the time had gone.

After her meeting with Asshole Conner, she had to put all of the energy she could into preparing for the investors' meeting and making the farm all that it could be. If it weren't for her agreement with Ros, she wouldn't be working on her large piece at all. The trails were coming along but still needed work.

She'd finished cleaning out another stall last night and ordered a dumpster after confirming a great deal of the stuff was junk. The salvageable stuff was packed away into two stalls to be sorted through when her cousins could make it out. Whatever they didn't want would be hauled away by local charities. The tack was sorted out and stored back in the tack room, where it should have been. It all needed to be cleaned, and some of it might not actually be salvageable. That particular task could wait, though.

If the upcoming meeting worked out as she hoped, and Ros had assured her repeatedly that it was likely, she'd be able to refinance and make her sabbatical permanent. With a great deal of luck, she'd have time to focus on her artwork after securing the financing. More likely, she'd get sucked into more work on the farm.

She winced at the thought. It felt disloyal, especially when she wanted the farm working again just as much as Sadie had. Regardless of the time she'd be able to put toward her art, there would be no more soul-crushing cases. The farm itself was a haven and would continue to be even if she didn't get as much time in the studio as she had dreamed. So why was she still so bummed?

Before she could put her finger on it, they were pulling into the county fairgrounds: home of the annual town picnic and many pleasant memories for her. Not as much for Liam. Exhaustion was painted all over his face.

"We haven't even started yet, babe." She winced internally as the endearment slipped out, but, fortunately for her sanity, he didn't appear to catch the slip.

Groaning, he rubbed his hands over his face before turning his head against the headrest to look at her. "Have you considered," he said slowly, "that I'm tired because you've been working me over like a dog with a bone?"

She propped her elbow against the window ledge of his car and rested her chin on her fist. "Oh, no, I hadn't realized your stamina had decreased so much. We should probably work on that."

He laughed loudly, eyes crinkling. Warmth spread through her at the sight. She'd always loved making him laugh. All too soon, he shook his head and shot her a fake grin. "Once more unto the breach," he said with a sigh.

She snorted. "You remember you're the reason we're here, yes?"

He raised both eyebrows. "Me? Who's the little miss destruction of property between the two of us?"

"You're bringing up destruction of property? You. The one who disabled my tractor with the sole purpose of getting me into trouble with the county." If he wanted an argument, she'd happily oblige. She could use the distraction too.

"You had my car towed without a single word," he growled.

"Oh, no. I wasn't done. You damaging my tractor was only the first bit of destruction of property, if you care to recall."

"Let's not get dramatic here. There was barely any damage."

Her mouth dropped open. "You could've burned my house down!"

"Almost only counts in horseshoes and hand grenades, sweetheart," he drawled.

Oh, good. She was back to wanting to throttle him. This was much more comfortable.

"Look," he said with a sigh, "did I know they would cause some disruption for your meeting? Yes, I had an idea. I had *no idea* it would be that *potentially* bad. And, I had no idea about the refinancing.

"You knew exactly what would happen with the dogs. Not to mention the goats. Wherever the hell *they* came from. The goats you obviously know something about."

"Potentially bad," she sputtered. "*Potentially*. Your potentially bad bullshit little stunt *actually* interfered with a meeting. If you hadn't sent those little hellions to wreak havoc, I could be presenting a business plan to a new loan officer right now. Not be here with you trying to save *your* career."

"Let's not pretend you're here for purely altruistic purposes," he muttered.

"I'm not pretending. I know exactly why I'm here. And, by the way, if I hypothetically had anything to do with the dogs while blinded by absolute rage over your stunt, I still would've taken basic precautions like a damn adult. You, on the other hand, lit a fucking match and waited to see what would burn."

He arched an eyebrow. "Oh, really? What precautions? Looked like plenty of damage from where I'm standing."

Turning to face him more fully, she crossed her arms. "Okay. So the dogs destroyed notes that weren't backed up? No. There were damaged books in your office, then? Ah, also no."

He shifted in the seat, eyeing her nervously. Good, he should be nervous.

"They got into your desk drawers, then? Or do you usually lock those drawers?"

His lips parted in surprise before he pressed them together into a thin line.

"And you weren't on thin ice with your boss because you've butted heads with other members of the department, showing a lack of ability to get along with others that was compounded by your reckless decision to post details about my private life to social media you use professionally?"

He blinked rapidly. "How did you find out about that?"

She rolled her eyes. "You and Ros don't have the market cornered on sources."

The thought of Ros brought her own mess back to the forefront of her mind. She sighed. Suddenly, all of her irritation with him was gone. She was too tired to argue with him.

He groaned, sinking down in the seat as he rubbed a hand over his eyes. "So you know..."

"That your boss wasn't looking to press charges for the dogs in your office? Yeah, I had an idea."

"Sorry?" he offered.

"Was that a question? Seriously?" she asked incredulously.

He gave her a self-deprecating grin. "It might have been, yeah."

"Why do I put up with you?"

His grin turned boyish. "My charming personality and dashing good looks?"

She scoffed. "Yeah, no. I don't think that's it."

He pursed his lips together. "The free labor, maybe."

She pointed at him. "That seems more likely, yeah."

He looked out the window toward the fairgrounds entrance. "So, once more unto the breach for the thing that's pretty much entirely my fault?"

She could live with that concession. "Sure. Try not to disable any of the rides or anything."

He laughed quietly. "Fair enough."

As they entered the gates, Leah felt herself unwind at the familiar faces and sights. She had missed this. It had been too long since she'd been to the Clearwater Annual Picnic. The event was part art festival, part food contest, and part county fair. It had been her favorite of the myriad festivals the town hosted. It wasn't advertised as heavily as the rest, making it a more townie-friendly event.

She took the lead in making the social rounds. If she had to be here with him, she was seeking out the people she wanted to see.

At the sound of her name being called in an excited tone, Leah whirled, accidentally smacking her shoulder hard against Liam's. She barely noticed his quiet grunt.

"Oh my God, girl, I thought that was you. How the hell have you been?"

Leah couldn't have stopped her smile if she tried. Marjorie Williams. She hadn't seen the other woman in years. They exchanged a tight hug. "I've been good. You?" Her voice matched Marjorie's own excitement.

"Good, good. I have my own cabin in Clearwater, so I get to be here whenever I want rather than just summers." Her brow furrowed with concern. "I heard about your aunt, Leah. I'm so sorry. She was a really amazing lady."

Leah smiled softly, ignoring the stab of pain caused by every offer of condolences. "Yeah, she really was. Thank you. Are you going to be in Clearwater long?"

"I'm actually heading back to the city tomorrow. I have a book launch party with some writing friends there."

Leah's face lit up. "Oh my God, Marj! You really did it? You're published?"

Marjorie squealed a little, dancing in place. "I did! I am! It took a lot of work, and I definitely funded the start of it through a more quote-unquote traditional job. Ugh, gag me. But, yes!

"I really love it, and better yet, I'm making enough to live on. Not earning as much as some out there, of course, but it's more than enough, and I want to keep loving it, you know?"

"I do." Leah returned Marjorie's smile. "Well, I get the idea, anyway."

"So, what are you doing back in Clearwater? Visiting or finally taking a break from the law job?"

"Yeah, I'm hoping it will turn into more than a break, but we'll see. I'm trying to get the farm back up to snuff, bring in a trainer, get the trails reopened."

Marjorie's face lit up with her excitement. "Aw, Lee. That's fantastic. I remember talking about all of the things you and Sadie wanted to do with the place. How's the art coming? That was a big part of what you were wanting, right?"

Leah forced a smile. "Haven't had as much time for it as I wanted, but I'm sure once I get through these next couple projects, I'll have more than enough time to focus on it."

She ignored Liam's frown and furrowed brows. "Don't you have an art show coming up, Lee?"

She blushed. Why did literally everything make her blush? "I do, but I already finished the pieces I need."

Marjorie glanced down at her wrist. "Oh, shit. I'm so sorry, but I am running *so* late. My girlfriend is waiting on me."

She held up her watch with a wince. "I apparently missed a few messages. I really want to catch up, though, and I very much want to hear about what you're doing with your art. And what's going on with the two of you. You were such a great couple back in the day. I'm glad to see you together again."

After entering her information into Leah's phone, she held Leah's gaze and squeezed her hand lightly. "Pursuing your passion is worth it, Lee.

Don't forget to live for your own dreams too."

Before Leah could think of a response or correct the assumption that they were *together* together, Marjorie was gone, her last words echoing in Leah's mind.

She was living for her own dream. Wasn't she? Yes. She'd wanted the same things as Sadie. She'd have more time for her art before she knew it. And Marjorie just didn't know her well enough anymore. She and Liam *had* been a really great couple, but they weren't together now. They wouldn't be good for each other now.

Shaking her head, she turned to Liam with a strained smile. "Well, that was quite the blast from the past."

He frowned, clearly unwilling to let the art thing go. "Rosalee told me you were working on a different piece, and the gallery owner was super excited about it. More so than the pieces you had already submitted. Did you finish it already?"

His arched brow told her he knew damn well she hadn't. There hadn't been enough time. She couldn't get it done now with everything else. Too much work needed to be done on the farm to get it ready for the next meeting. The new time crunch made it more important than ever.

She did not want to have this conversation with him. The stubborn expression on his face told her he wouldn't be letting it go anytime soon. She groaned.

"The pieces I already have for the show will be fine. Yes, it would have been awesome if I could have gotten this one done in time, but it's hardly the end of the world. The farm has a deadline; my art doesn't."

Liam crossed his arms. "Sadie talked about this show constantly these last few months. She was convinced it would be the break you need. Something that could set you up with commissions for years, and the sale for the piece alone would be a significant nest egg."

She stepped back from him, crossing her arms over her chest. Why wouldn't he let this go? Yes, Sadie had been excited about the possibilities. Sadie probably also thought she'd have time to pay down the mortgage herself.

"I will have another shot at my art," she said firmly. "I won't have another shot at bringing the farm back to what it could be. I want to keep this farm more than anything. I want it to thrive again. It has a price tag, and I'm going to do everything I can to make sure I can pay it."

"Yes," he ground out, "a price tag that selling your piece could take care of."

She rolled her eyes. "I'm not gambling the farm on a pipe dream. Sadie had way more faith in that piece than I can afford right now."

"Sadie wouldn't want you throwing away your dream for hers."

She wanted to scream with frustration. Why did people keep assuming she was living Sadie's dream? It was her dream too.

"I'm not throwing away my dream, Liam. How many times do I have to say this? The art can wait. If the right person sees the farm as cleaned up as I can get it, they're a surer bet than making it as an artist. Sadie was biased. She thought I could do anything, but she isn't here."

She took in a shaky breath. "Regardless, it's none of your business." She looked away, hating the pity she saw on his face. Almost as much as the stubbornness shining through. He wasn't going to let this go.

"I'm going to the bathroom. Meet you at the buffet?" She walked away before he could respond, wiping her eyes discreetly.

She was letting the water trickle out from her cupped hands. Focusing on the steady trickle was soothing her as much as washing her face with the cool water had.

The sight of another person immediately behind her in the mirror made her jump with a shriek.

"Oh, crap, Leah, I'm sorry. I didn't mean to scare you."

She braced her hands against the sink, taking steady breaths. "Shannon, hey," Leah said, forcing a smile. "No worries. I was just distracted."

Shannon returned her smile.. "Hey, how are you doing with everything?"

"Doing okay. The farm is more challenging than I initially anticipated, but I think it's really coming together. Liam and Byron have been a really huge help. I wouldn't have made anywhere near this progress without them, plus all of the help that Byron scrounged up."

Shannon bit her lip. "About Liam," she said slowly, "I hope you don't think I'm overstepping, and I don't want you to take this the wrong way, but I'm concerned."

Leah snagged a towel to dry her hands. "I'm not sure what you mean."

"Well, it's just that... He didn't have the best upbringing." Gesturing at Leah, she added, "Which you know already, of course. It's just. You know that a boy pulling your pigtails isn't an appropriate way to tell you that he likes you, right?"

"Um..." What? Her brain was filled with white noise. She was not expecting Shannon to go there. Shaking her head, she forced herself to say something, anything.

"Uh, yeah. I know, and that's really not what this is. He's making it up to me. And he definitely didn't post that to get my attention. Besides, it's not like it costs me anything to give him a chance to make up for it. Whatever he was thinking, he's working on making it right. And it's not like I did nothing."

Shannon smiled tightly. "Just be careful, dear. The Devlin boys have always been a lot, and I don't want to see you get burned again."

"Right." Shannon was trying to be helpful. She did not deserve Leah's irritation. Or, more likely, she was simply being nosy and looking for gossip. Her motivation was beside the point. She was not going to snap at her.

"Thanks for your concern, Shannon. We've simply agreed to bury the hatchet. It's not like we're dating again."

"Of course," she responded. She gave Leah a motherly smile, setting Leah's teeth on edge. She *had* a mother. One who had enough opinions about Leah's life. She didn't need more input.

Fortunately, a group of women came in, affording Leah the opportunity to wave and smile before ducking out and losing Shannon in the crowd.

Chapter Thirteen: The Storm

"You should go, get some work done."

Leah dusted off her hands before waving them around at the scene. They'd been clearing brush off the trails with Byron's crew since early that morning. "Is this not working?"

He rolled his eyes. "You know what I mean. Rosalee has been riding me about making sure you're holding up your end of the deal."

She crossed her arms, narrowing her eyes at Liam. So this was the latest tactic. They were ganging up on her. "You've been talking to Ros?"

He sighed before tossing another log into the modified trailer behind the side-by-side. "I'd say it's more Rosalee talking to me, but yes. Her connections extend to some people on the tenure committee."

"Oh, now I see. That's what this whole pushing me on the art thing is about. Ros put a bug in your ear."

"What?" He shook his head, brow furrowed. "No. Well, yes, she has talked to me about it. But that has nothing to do with our conversation yesterday."

"Okay," she agreed. If she doubted his motivations enough, maybe he'd let it go.

He raised his hands into the air. "Believe me or not. I'm saying we've got this covered, and you have an agreement with Rosalee to uphold. Go, get some work done on your piece. Find joy, or whatever."

She returned to clearing the brush. She could feel his eyes on her, but she studiously ignored him. Looking anywhere but at him, she steadily loaded the trailer with the overgrowth Byron's team had already trimmed for them to haul out.

"So you're just going to ignore me?"

She shrugged. "I don't like being told what to do." More time to work on her piece sounded great, but she couldn't abandon the team that was out here for free to help her out. Not giving him the satisfaction was a bonus.

"Alright. Fair enough. You don't want me telling you what to do. So, despite the fact that we've clearly got this handled, Byron's team is having the time of their lives, and you've got my labor already procured, you're just going to stay out here. Because, what? I made the suggestion?"

She turned to face him. "That wasn't a suggestion. Don't you teach English? Shouldn't you know the difference between a command and a suggestion?"

He rolled his eyes. "It was absolutely a suggestion. Don't make me quote myself."

"That's fine. I'll quote you. 'Go, get some work done.'" She used finger quotes. She had to bite her lips to keep from laughing at his expression.

He heaved a sigh. "Seriously? That's not how I said it. And you're ignoring the fact this conversation started with a *suggestion* of what you *should do* because you have all of the help you need. The two main trails you wanted cleared are already cleared. This is just bonus. And it's something you want to do anyway."

He had a point. "I can't just leave everyone out here."

"Yeah, you can. They're not doing it just for you, and I'm certainly not doing this just for you. So, what's the holdup? Need me to call Rosalee to talk some sense into you? I can do that."

Her mouth dropped open. "You wouldn't dare."

He cocked an eyebrow, smirk sliding into place. "Sweetheart, you really don't know me, if you think that's true."

Dammit. She did know him, and he definitely would. If he was telling the truth about discussing the tenure situation with Ros in the first place, then he would absolutely rat her out. Ros would appreciate it. Leah did not need the lecture, and she *did* want to work on her piece.

When his hand snaked toward his pocket, she huffed and threw her hands up in surrender. "Fine. You win. I'm going."

"Fabulous."

She wanted to wipe the smug grin off his face, but she was absolutely not restarting the war they'd just settled. Even if there was a tempting mud puddle sitting right there that would make a phenomenal projectile.

Hours later, she jumped when the radio in her studio blared out an alarm. Turning the sound up, her brows furrowed as her lips turned down. A storm warning. The meteorologist anticipated a tornado warning would be issued within the next couple of hours. She had to get everyone home.

Liam ducked into the cabin, the wind blowing in hard behind him until he forced the door closed. He chafed his hands together and glanced at her through the hair falling into his eyes. "The horses are handled. They'll be able to get out if they feel the need."

"Great, thanks. You ready to head down?" She nodded toward the cabin's trapdoor into the basement.

He shook his head. "I'm going to head home."

Oh, fun. He was going the stubborn dumbass route. "Liam, there's a tornado warning. Bad enough you didn't leave with Byron's crew when the storm started. Report says there's at least two on the radar now. You can't be on the road."

He shrugged. "It's not far, Leah. I'll be fine."

She ran her hands through her hair before letting them drop to her sides. "Seriously, Liam? It's not far?"

His stance firmed.

She clenched her jaw. Of course he was going to be difficult about this. "Please, just come down to the basement with me. Don't make me worry about you getting home."

He narrowed his eyes. "I see what you're doing."

"Yeah, well, your family has the worst fucking luck. I will absolutely stoop to manipulation to avoid tempting fate."

He cast her a quick flash of a grin and a wink. "It's almost like you care about me or something."

She widened her eyes with faux innocence. "Where else am I going to get free labor?"

He laughed softly. "Alright, you win." He nodded toward the trapdoor. "I'll follow you down."

Once at the bottom, she turned on the light. Her lips curved into a grin when Sadie's painted ceiling was illuminated. Double-checking that all of the supplies were in place, she motioned him down.

Watching him come down the ladder, her lips parted. Seriously, how did he get more attractive over time? When he tugged the heavy trapdoor down, she watched the play of muscles under his damp shirt. She stepped back with a blush when he dropped to the floor and turned.

His smirk told her he definitely caught her.

She spread her hands and shrugged. "Sorry for enjoying the view?"

Laughing, he shook his head. "Now who's making statements into questions?"

She spread her hands. "Not trying to seduce you, promise."

"I won't hold it against you," he murmured.

Her traitorous mind popped up an offer of what he could hold against her. She reminded herself he didn't have sex without feelings, and she'd already decided feelings were off the table. She refused to acknowledge the tiny voice saying feelings were already present. He didn't feel the same, anyway. Shoving the dirty, and traitorous, thoughts into the mental corner where they belonged, she grinned. "Appreciate it."

Squeezing behind her, he entered the large space away from the ladder. He settled into one of the small couches, extending his long legs out in front of him. His eyes twinkled in the light as a slow smile spread across his face. "I'll let you in on a secret, if you give me one in exchange."

She studied him in turn before settling into the second small couch, pulling her knees up against her chest and tugging the small throw she had tossed down there earlier around her shoulders. "Wow. I haven't even thought about that game in years."

"Going to need to pass the time somehow, right?"

"And out of all of the ways we could pass the time, you pick that one? The one that has gotten us into the weirdest and most intimate conversations ever?"

He grinned, unrepentant. "Most people would tell you poking at something is just my nature."

"Most people would," she agreed. "Alright, let's hear it. What's your truth?"

"What if I want you to seduce me?"

Her mouth went dry as her heart rate kicked up. She grabbed a water bottle and took a sip before looking back at him. "That's not a statement."

His lips quirked up into a half smile. "Fair point. I would be interested in seduction," he said slowly.

"I am... not entirely sure what to do with that."

He raised a hand and beckoned with two fingers in a *give it here* gesture. "Your turn."

She leaned her chin on her knees, feeling like a teenager again as butterflies danced in her stomach. What were they doing? "I would be interested in pursuing that avenue."

She sighed, looking away again. "But I don't think either of us could afford it."

His smile dimmed. "I'm not entirely sure what to do with that."

She laughed, rolling her eyes at the pair they made. "First question's yours, then."

He shifted to lie across the couch with his legs propped up on the wall. Folding his arm beneath his head, he gazed up at the night sky Sadie had painted across the ceiling.

"Alright. What was your shittiest breakup?"

She raised her eyebrows. "Going straight for the jugular tonight. Okay. If that's how you want to play it."

He gave her a boyish grin but said nothing.

"College boyfriend, Kevin Fahrland. I walked in on him having sex with my roommate, Dolly."

"Dolly," he said, looking over at her to arch an eyebrow.

She shrugged. "Her mom really liked country."

"But didn't you say...?"

"Nope, no commenting on the truthing, no follow-up questions, and your turn is over."

He pushed his lower lip out in a fake pout. "We're still following that rule?"

"Yes, sir, we are. Unless you'd like to make a change to the rule book.

In which case, I would be willing to entertain a motion." She pushed fake glasses up her nose.

He studied her with narrowed eyes, clearly weighing the pros and cons of eliminating what had ultimately been his favorite, or at least most utilized, rule. "Nah, no motion."

She wondered briefly if she really wanted to ask the question on the tip of her tongue. With a sigh, she threw caution to the wind. "Why did you break up with me?"

He was silent so long she thought he'd forfeit.

"Carol told me, among other things, that I was standing in the way of the realization of your potential. That you would squander every last drop of potential and settle for less than you deserved. That being with me would cost you every opportunity, and I was absolutely not a suitable consolation prize for lost opportunities."

Leah sucked in a sharp breath.

"Eventually, maybe not in a year or even two, but eventually, you would resent me holding you back. I was bound to lose you because a boy like me had no business with a girl like you."

She swallowed harshly. Her throat felt so tight. What had her mother *done*? How could she?

"The very next day, you told me you applied to the community college in the city, and you'd decided to defer your acceptance to your first choice school. Which was all the confirmation I thought I needed to know she was right." He cast her a self-deprecating grin before returning his gaze to the ceiling.

"There you were throwing away the chance to go to a good college, get a decent education, and do something more with your life. So, that was that."

"Liam…"

"No commenting allowed, sweetheart."

She groaned. At least now she knew. "Fair's fair, I guess. Your turn."

"Why didn't you come back?"

She sighed, slumping back into the couch to study the ceiling. She wondered, briefly, what would have happened if she had come back sooner. If she'd returned after law school like she'd planned, would they have started something all over again?

"At first, I wanted to avoid the site of my oh-so-tragic teen romance."

He laughed at her glib tone.

"Sadie, of course, cajoled me back, and I was here for the bulk of my college summers. And then," she sighed, "law school. Internships every summer for the résumé. Then, studying for the bar exam. Barely left my apartment. My roommate and I almost killed each other. Cannot tell you how badly I wished Dolly went to law school with me."

She caught the arched eyebrow out of the corner of her eye and shrugged. "That is an answer to an entirely different question. Back here for a month after the bar exam, during which time I never left the farm.

"And then, I started at the firm, decided to really give it my all for a while, make the cost worth it. I barely had time to breathe, much less make it out here for much more than the holidays until a couple of years in. It was not a great time," she added, laughing at herself.

"The weekend before Sadie's heart attack, we stayed up all night putting together some alternate plans. It's what I used as my pitch at the meeting." She rubbed her eyes, pushing the gathered moisture out and wiping it off on her sleeves.

After she'd gathered herself, Liam reminded her it was her turn to ask.

"Why didn't you leave?" He'd talked about getting out, seeing the world beyond Clearwater.

"I probably should've expected that."

"You probably should have," she agreed archly.

"Hell, Lee, I don't know."

"Bullshit," she said softly. "You started it. Forfeit or answer."

He took a deep breath. "I didn't want to leave my brother. I didn't want my dad to ruin any more of my life than he already had, and I wasn't willing to track down Mom when she didn't bother to keep in touch with me. So, I left, I got my degree, and I came back. I think I even managed to sway the overall Devlin reputation until that stupid post."

She raised her eyebrows, wondering how much progress they'd managed to make in walking back said stupid post.

"No word yet on how my tenure chances are looking. Rosalee thinks another few sightings of the two of us, either showing me groveling as expected or you graciously accepting my plea for forgiveness will cool the remaining ire. And I have to participate in more town togetherness."

Looking over at her, he arched an eyebrow in question. "Did you tell her about our deal?"

"No," Leah answered, lips curling into a smirk, "I didn't tell her."

"Ah, hell." He slapped his hand over his eyes and groaned.

She grinned. "In the interests of giving you a little more bang for your wasted buck of a question, I have told Cassidy, Paige, and Derek. Nobody else heard it from me."

"Of course you told your cousins."

"Are you going to try to tell me you expected anything different?"

He scoffed, shaking his head. "Nah. You're really going to consider that my turn?"

"Yes," she answered smugly, "but I'm not going to count that stupid ass question."

"How gracious of you," he muttered.

"Indeed," she agreed archly. Should she ask the question she wanted to ask, or let him off the hook? Rolling her eyes at herself, she decided to be fair. "Have you told anyone?"

He laughed. "That's sweet, but you know I haven't. So ask your actual question."

"Why'd you write the post?"

He sighed and sat up, rubbing his face with both hands. Finally looking at her, he shook his head. "Forfeit."

Huh. She... was not expecting that. If it had been as simple as irritation going overboard as it had with her, or Alec needling, or him drinking and doing something stupid, he wouldn't have forfeited. He knew the forfeit alone was a tell. One she'd used shamelessly in the past to end the game faster without using a forfeit herself.

He stood and walked over to turn on the radio. In short order, the announcer reported the tornado warning was still in effect for the county. He glanced from the single platform bed to her before offering to sleep on the couches.

"Don't be ridiculous," she said, rolling her eyes. "You barely fit on the couch. You would end up on the concrete. We're both adults the last time I checked. We can share the bed. There should be some sweats in that box for you to sleep in."

When he shook his head, she deliberately misinterpreted his objection. "Promise I'll avert my eyes."

"Leah," he sighed.

"Hey now," she said, "don't act like I'm the one being unreasonable." After grabbing a lantern from the table between the couches, she clicked it on and walked over to the bed. Climbing under the covers, she added, "Can you get the light when you're done over there?"

He rolled his eyes but nodded, giving in.

Turning to face the wall as promised, she listened to him dig through the box for comfortable clothing. Fabric rustled against skin as he changed out of his jeans and into whatever comfortable clothing he could find in the box. Then, the snick of the string turning off the overhead light. The domesticity of the quiet sounds sent a pang of longing through her. She sighed quietly, burying her face in the pillow.

A quick draft of chill air sent a shiver down her spine. He slid under the covers but carefully left space between them. She giggled, trying and failing to muffle the sound against her pillow.

"Shut up," he muttered.

Her giggle turned into a full-blown laugh. When she calmed, she wiped the moisture from the corners of her eyes. "Do you happen to recall that conversation not so long ago? The one where we both agreed that some form of seduction, leading to so much touching, was on both of our minds. And regardless of the whole *will we, won't we*, we are both adults, fully capable of keeping our paws to ourselves."

When he remained silent, she shook her head, laughing softly. "When's the last time you shared a bed with someone, anyway?"

He was quiet so long she thought he'd decided to ignore her. Eventually, he sighed before moving to close the comically wide gap that had left him hanging halfway off the bed. "Forfeit."

She resisted the strong urge to poke at him. She'd just finished reminding him they were both adults. Besides, she was exhausted. Feeling safer than she had in ages, she quickly fell asleep to the sound of Liam's steady breathing.

Chapter Fourteen: Shelter

A loud crash outside startled her awake. Lying in the dark, she reoriented herself, running through her five senses and replaying the events of the night before until her heartbeat calmed. When she landed on touch, she felt something was missing. Where was Liam? Frowning, she reached out until she grazed his side, farther away than should have been possible given his size.

Sitting up, she felt her way to the bottom of the bed and reached down to the floor to pick up the lantern. When light flooded the space, she slammed her eyes closed then squinted until she could adjust. Her heart clenched at the sight of Liam curled tightly in the corner of the bed, his arms corded with tension.

Shit. She called his name, increasing her volume with each repetition. Nothing. She bit her lip, debating between leaving him like that or touching him. When a nearby bolt of lightning shook the cabin above them, he curled tighter, brow furrowing. Yeah, she wasn't going to leave him to the nightmares. She clasped his ankle lightly, shaking him and calling his name again. At the combination, he flinched violently, scrambling up against the headboard, hands raised in front of his face. Her stomach twisted painfully at the sight.

She watched his chest heave in silence, giving him space to finish coming out of it. His arms came down first, leaving him blinking into the sudden light.

"Thanks," he said, voice raspy.

"Sure thing."

Straightening his legs out in front of him, he winced at the stretch to overtaxed muscles. He leaned his head back against the wall with a groan, closing his eyes before taking several deep breaths.

When his gaze settled back on her, she gave him a grim smile. "Still happen often?"

"No, it's been a while," he answered, rubbing his eyes. He gave her a tired smile. "Therapy for the win."

"How long have you been seeing someone?"

"Off and on since college. You?"

"Off and on since college." She followed his gaze back to the stars painted on the ceiling.

"Do you want to talk about it?" she asked hesitantly.

He grinned, flicking his eyes back to her. "Therapy?"

She rolled her eyes and nudged him with her foot. "Not what I meant but sure."

He was silent for several minutes, but it was a comfortable quiet. "Dad called me the night I wrote that post."

When she winced, he nodded. "Apparently, the anniversary had him feeling nostalgic this time around."

Of course that would be the anniversary his father chose to acknowledge.

Sadie had been hosting Mrs. Devlin and her children for a sleepover at the farmhouse, ostensibly so the kids could hang out and have a cozily spooky night during the storm. That was the story Liam's younger brother, Henry, and sister, Eliza, were given, anyway. It would have been more accurate to say Anna Devlin was seeking shelter from her husband.

When he called her phone several times within the space of a few minutes, Sadie suggested she turn her phone off. Anna refused. "I'll just answer. Let him know we're fine and spending some time here. He's probably just worried."

On her way back to the living room where they were all spread out, Leah heard enough of the phone call. Enough to hear Marcus Devlin call Leah a little whore, Anna an incompetent mother, and Sadie an evil temptress. Before she was caught eavesdropping, she returned to the main room, retaking her place in front of the sofa with Liam, his arm settling back around her shoulders before drawing her closer to his side.

Anna had returned to the room several minutes later, packed up her children, and left, deaf to Sadie's protests that it wasn't safe to be driving in the storm. Rain and the inky black night made visibility terrible. Anna had assured her that Marcus felt it would be just fine. The drive was short. When Sadie suggested she at least leave the children behind where it was safe and dry, Anna refused. Marcus wanted his wife and children back home.

Hours later, Marcus Devlin woke Leah and Sadie, pounding on the cabin door and screaming at them for getting his boy killed. Leah would find out later that Anna's car had been hit by a driver who had hydroplaned out of control and slid into her lane. He had struck the driver's side, killing

Henry instantly and seriously injuring Anna. Eliza had minor scrapes. Liam walked away without physical injuries.

"So, yeah, he called."

She watched him closely, hands stilling against the comforter. "Shit."

His mouth twisted into a sardonic smile. "He's back in prison, and I shouldn't have accepted the call. I mean really," he gestured with his hands, "I definitely knew better.

"He blamed me for Henry, of course. The only worthwhile son dead because I had to see my girlfriend. Same song, different verse. Then, he moved on to telling me it's my fault he lost his wife and daughter. You see, Mom didn't leave because he was beating the shit out of her. Nah, that was all me."

"Jesus, Liam."

"No commentary allowed," he said softly. "So, that's the answer to your last question. Dad was his typical self, and I regressed. I am sorry you were in the line of fire, by the way. I don't actually expect you to forgive me, but I am sorry."

She rolled her eyes. "Sorry to blow your expectations, but I forgive you. I haven't actually thought about the post in a while. Or the dogs," she paused, head cocked to the side. "Or the tractor, come to think of it."

She laughed at his disbelieving expression. "Not going to lie, I was absolutely furious with you. But there's been too much going on to really focus on something like that."

He shook his head.

"What?"

"You shouldn't…"

At her raised eyebrow, he shrugged defensively. "Look, I'm not trying to tell you how to feel, but it seems like you shouldn't forgive me just like that."

She laughed. "Oh, come on. It's not *just like that*. Frankly, I've been taking advantage of you."

He rolled his eyes. "I would've done the same work and more for Sadie, anyway. Or for you, if I'd known about the mortgage issues. I offered to help her with most of those projects at one point or another. It's not a big deal."

"Yeah, alright," she agreed sarcastically, "you haven't been a huge help. My mistake."

His lips tipped up into a half-smile, and she knew she'd won this round.

"It took me some time, but, yeah, I do forgive you. And regardless of whether you think you deserve it, I do believe *I* get to decide when to forgive as the wronged party."

"Does this mean no more hard labor?" His eyes twinkled as he fought a smile.

"Ha, no. You're not getting out of it that easily. Unless you don't need *my* help anymore?"

"Nope, definitely still need your shining presence to butter up my boss tomorrow."

"Good. I have not a fucking clue what I'd do without the barter system labor."

"About that," he said slowly.

"Yes?" she asked carefully.

"I talked to a friend of mine in the forestry program at the community college. He's got some students looking for field credits, and Byron has expressed interest in supervising. Apparently, he taught forest management for several years. Byron thinks they'd be able to clear out all of the trails before your next meeting with the extra help. Maybe even cut some new paths into the state land. I can focus on the barn, then, so you can focus on finishing that piece."

"You're kidding." Her mouth opened and closed as she tried to process.

"Nope. I'll send you the contact info in the morning. He just needs confirmation that you're on board. He can settle the rest of the details with Byron. Byron is stoked at the idea of educating young minds again. I'm sure he's going to rope all of them into his club."

She squealed, launching herself across the bed to hug him. "Oh my God, Liam, thank you, thank you, thank you."

His arms circled her, and she knew everything would be okay. When she sat back, he trailed his arms down her sides to encircle her waist. His gaze flicked from her eyes to her lips, and she found herself similarly distracted. She pulled her lips into her mouth, wetting them. She leaned into his palm when he reached up to cradle the side of her face. Leaning down, she braced herself with one hand against the headboard and cupped his face with the other. Sparks ignited, and warmth suffused her body when their lips finally met.

She moaned before pulling herself away. He looked equally dazed. Her lips curled into a smile. Eyes dancing, she raised an eyebrow. "Yeah?"

He held up a finger and moved her back enough to fish into his jeans for his wallet. Pulling out a condom, he grinned triumphantly. His grin turned wicked when they settled back into their starting positions. "Yeah."

Slipping her hands under his shirt, she traced her fingertips along his side, slowly dragging his shirt up until he growled and jerked it off himself. His broad hands grasped her waist, thumbs dragging under her shirt to stroke against her heated skin. She squeaked when he pulled her forward, drawing her legs around his waist. She might have spared a moment to be embarrassed about the noise, if her thoughts weren't occupied with *holy shit, hot.*

She stared down at him, feeling almost breathless with want at the sight of her own need reflected back at her. Cupping his face in her hands, she pulled him into an achingly slow kiss. Liquid heat pooled in her core. She wanted, *needed* more. When his tongue flicked against her lips, she gasped and let him in. Arms banding behind her back, he pulled her impossibly closer.

Her core tightened at the too light friction provided by the band of his pants. Liam pushed her hair back to place open-mouthed kisses down her neck. She bared her neck for him, pulling her hair in front of her opposite shoulder. When he pulled her shirt to bare more of her neck, tongue flicking out lightly before moving to her right collarbone, she moaned. His tongue dipped into the hollow of her throat before he trailed feather-light kisses back up the other side of her neck, pushing her hair out of his way.

Seeking more sensation, she dragged her nails down his back lightly before tracing along the top of his pants. When he drew his teeth lightly against her neck, she groaned, squeezing his ass beneath the sweats. He echoed her, tightening his grip around her waist.

How did she forget how *good* he was at this? *Shit.* Her shirt needed to be off, now. He'd have to stop. But then he'd have more access. Why was she letting him have all of the fun anyway? A particularly fortunate flick of his tongue behind her ear sent a trail of liquid heat straight to her core. *Right.* That was why.

She pushed him back lightly to pull off her shirt, the motion a far cry for her typical smooth disrobing. He drank in her newly bared skin, pupils blown wide with arousal. The man could make a nun question her vows. Oh good, her turn.

Before he could distract her from her new mission, she pushed against his broad shoulders. He followed her direction easily, lowering himself back to the bed until he was laid out beneath her like the best kind of feast. Her mouth watered. Whatever past Leah did in her former lives to deserve this, the woman deserved *all of the flowers*. Bracing herself with a hand by his head, she leaned down for another kiss.

She moaned again when his calloused hands dragged down her back to cup her ass beneath her pants. She trailed her own hands down his sides, thumbs gliding along the ridges of his abs as she did. She felt drunk on desire, thoughts slow as molasses while her heart rabbited in her chest.

His hands dragged back up along her spine when she abandoned his mouth to bite lightly at his neck. She took shameless advantage of the greater access when he dropped his head back with a groan. She twirled her tongue around his nipple before biting down gently, his soft curses music to her ears. His hips jerked, almost unseating her, when she flicked one nipple while biting the other. Pulling back, she laughed wickedly and kissed him lightly before continuing her slow descent.

"You don't—" his voice was raspy, breaking off when she traced his hip bone.

Looking up his body, she found his eyes already locked on her. "I don't?"

His throat bobbed. "You don't have to..." He cut himself off, gesturing.

She laughed. "I know. But I *want*." She tugged on the waistband. "Off, please."

He cursed again before pushing them down. Her eyes zeroed in on his cock, and she smiled like the cat that got the canary. Holding his gaze, she took him in hand before darting her tongue out to lick from root to tip.

He breathed out shakily. "*Fuck*, that feels good."

Delight coursed through her as she repeated the action more slowly, tongue swirling. She had always loved watching her partner fall apart in bed. Something about making him tremble with pleasure was *better*. Slipping her hand beneath her own waistband, she dipped her fingers into her core. Shuddering, she braced her forehead against his thigh as she gave in to temptation and flicked her thumb against her clit.

Pulling her wet fingers back out, she found herself falling into his eyes. He'd propped the pillows up behind him. His eyes seared her, making her clench around nothing.

"*Fucking hell,*" he groaned, head falling back.

She moved up to kiss him, bracing her opposite hand against his chest for leverage. He jerked like she shocked him when she wrapped her wet fingers around his cock. She laughed throatily at his dazed expression before returning to her earlier task.

She worked his cock with her arousal-wet fingers before closing her mouth over the tip of him. She locked eyes with him again before sliding her mouth down. Gentleman that he was, he held himself back from fucking up into her throat, but he couldn't stop the minute jerking as she bobbed up and down his cock.

"Get back up here."

She arched an eyebrow, sliding off him with a light pop and sitting back up to straddle him again. She exaggerated a pout, widening her eyes as she did. "Are you not enjoying yourself?"

"What? Of *course* I'm—" he cut himself off with a soft curse when she went down on him again. She enjoyed herself while he made the effort to gather his scattered thoughts again.

"Fucking hell, Leah," he groaned, tugging lightly on her hair. She sat up; she could be nice and let the poor man gather his thoughts. Her capacity for benevolence only extended so far, however. His mouth gaped when she played with her breasts, pushing them together before running a wet finger around each nipple.

He swallowed harshly before shaking his head. "I've been dreaming about your pussy, and I think I've been patient long enough."

She trailed her fingers from her breast to her core. She circled her clit lightly before she pressed her fingers back into her wet center. Her head fell back with a moan. Drawing her fingers back out, she rubbed her thumb against her wet fingers before casting him a look of false innocence. "This pussy?"

She barely got the words out before he lifted her up his body, settling her back down with her knees bracketing his head.

"Yeah," he rasped, "that pussy."

He caressed her hip bones, dragging his thumbs back and forth. She braced a hand against the wall when the simple sensation sent tingles down her thighs. Her hips twitched forward as she clenched around nothing.

"There's my girl," he said, voice rough.

She laughed softly, and he gave her a wolfish grin before pulling her forward. His tongue darted out, tracing along her outer lips before dipping between the folds. The slow drag of his tongue up and down her outer labia made her gasp. His tongue's slow exploration drove her higher. When he blew a light stream of air over her opening, she twitched forward with a curse.

Bending her arm against the wall, she rested her forehead against it, looking down between their bodies. Fuck, he knew what he was doing. He played her like an instrument, taking his time alternating between quick flicks of his tongue to her clit and slow drags over her inner lips until she was a writhing mess above him.

When he'd driven her to the edge, he focused broader strokes of his tongue over her clit until she tipped over. Her legs tightened around his head, and she gasped a harsh exhale through the overwhelming crush of pleasure. As she came down, she felt him making broad strokes around her outer lips again, drawing out the aftershocks until she tipped over to his side.

She vaguely heard his murmur of protest. Patting him drunkenly, she slurred, "So good."

He laughed before capturing her hand, laying soft kisses against each fingertip before releasing her.

She lay next to him, panting like a racehorse, relishing the feeling of minor muscle groups contracting and releasing down her legs with the aftershocks of pleasure. Staring at the ceiling for long moments, she blinked dazedly until she made it back down to Earth. Clumsily, she patted his side before turning her head to face him.

She couldn't fault the smug grin he wore. His lips tipped up into a broader smile, and she grinned back at him.

"Yes, dear?" he asked, eyes dancing.

"Still have that condom?"

His eyes darkened with renewed arousal before he nodded. Her mouth watered as she watched him put it on. Yeah, she was definitely ready for round two. He braced himself over her body, staring down at her with a look of wonder on his face.

She pushed the hair out of his eyes, tucking it behind his ear before cupping the side of his face. He kissed her palm, darting his tongue out in a quick lick that sent a wet pulse of heat through her core.

The hair fell into his eyes again when he lowered himself to kiss her languidly. She moaned, tucking her leg around him to pull him closer. He obliged, pressing more of his weight into her, kissing her until they were both breathless.

Pushing himself up to hover above her, he grinned down at her. She could imagine the sight she made. Flush crept down her chest as heat suffused every limb. Eyes tracing down his body held above her, she bit her lip.

Shifting his weight to brace against one hand, he pulled the other down her side. His thumb brushed against her sensitive nipple, making her twitch. He bent to draw the nub into his mouth. Her hand slid into his hair, holding him in place as he swirled his tongue around the pink bud. His hand continued its slow drag down her body until he slid two fingers into her.

She was so wet, his fingers slid in with little sensation, but his thumb brushing against her clit more than made up for it. The hand in his hair clenched tight as she arched, pulling a moan from him.

When she forced her hand to relax a fraction, he used the slack to switch to her other nipple. Twirling his tongue around the opposite bud, he slid a third finger into her.

"Liam, fuck," she moaned. "I'm not going to last, if you keep…" He pulled another moan from her when he twisted his fingers inside her.

He pulled off her nipple and flicked his gaze up to her. "Sorry. What was that?"

She yanked lightly on his hair in retaliation, and he gave her an unrepentant grin. His fingers curled inside her again, circling that perfect spot, and she yanked hard, lost in the sensation. Tingles raced up and down her legs in time with the slow glide of his fingers. When he bent his attention back to her nipples, she was lost. Sparks burst behind her eyes as she tipped over into her second orgasm, spasming around his fingers as her mouth dropped open with a gasp. He slowed his pace, dragging out the sensation until she writhed against the sheets.

When she finished blinking the black spots from her vision, she found him resting against her abdomen as he drew random designs against her side with his fingers. Her fingers were still tangled in his hair.

Noticing her attention, he grinned slowly, heat simmering in his gaze. Her core spasmed, making her groan at the new sparks of heat dancing through her.

She tugged his hair lightly. "You're going to kill me."

"Oh, but what a way to go," he said, shit-eating grin firmly in place as he rose up to hover over her again.

"What a way to go," she agreed, laughter dancing in her eyes.

He kissed her slowly, and she marveled at his patience. Her hand skated clumsily along his side before dipping to wrap around his length.

His hips stuttered forward as he bent his forehead to rest against hers, panting. Their eyes locked, and she stroked up lightly. He closed his eyes, savoring the sensation.

"We should probably do something about this," she said.

When he opened his eyes again, she found herself lost in his gaze. He reached up, brushing a strand of hair out of her eyes tenderly. She hadn't felt this close to anyone ever.

She guided him to her, gasping when she felt him slide home. Here was the friction she'd been craving. Running her hands down his back, she stopped at his ass, pulling him into her to pick up the pace. She pulled one foot up next to his hip, allowing him to slide deeper into her with a muffled curse.

"Yes," she said, voice breathy. "Just like that."

Bless the man, he actually obliged with the pace. Changing only his angle until she gasped, back arching, when he brushed across her G-spot. He stilled inside her briefly, waiting until her eyes met his again. His grin was positively feral.

"Unfair."

He laughed softly, making them both shudder at the sensation. "What is?"

She shook her head slowly, maintaining eye contact. "You are just..." She groaned before pulling him down into a kiss.

Her fingernails dug into his back when he resumed his prior pace, hitting her G-spot with each perfect thrust. She arched up to meet him, her earlier exhaustion forgotten. In short order, a rush of pleasure spread through her, and she spasmed around him, pulling him over the edge with her.

Leah stretched slowly when she woke, smiling when she brushed against Liam. Turning to her side to face him, her smile grew at his sleepy expression.

"Morning," he said roughly.

"Good morning." Her voice was sappy, and she couldn't muster up the energy to care.

He yawned, rubbing his face against his bent arm. "Sleep well?"

"Mmm," she hummed. She hadn't slept that well in years. "Very. You?"

He nodded, eyes twinkling with his smile. "You ready to face the world?"

"Ugh," she groaned, hiding her face in her pillow. "No. Let's not and say we didn't."

He laughed. "The horses aren't going to feed themselves."

"Hmm," she murmured, turning her face to look back at him, "that sounds like a you problem."

"Oh, it does, does it?" Her eyes caught on the wrinkles carved into the corners of his eyes from his smile.

She nodded, grinning smugly at his arched eyebrow.

"I suppose I can handle that. Does calling the college to settle up the final details to get a bunch of gung-ho forestry students out here sound like a you problem?"

She groaned, burying her head in the pillow.

"Forestry students who will expedite cleaning out all of the existing trails and probably even mark out and open up new ones for you." His voice was smug. She'd find more energy to care about it if she weren't still sleep-warm and lazy from the night before.

Her voice was muffled by the pillow when she spoke again. "Ugh, yes. That does sound like a me problem. Sounds like a me problem that can wait until I take a shower, though."

He grabbed his watch from the small table next to the bed. "Well, if we, excuse me, *I*, make the animals wait any longer, they're likely to stage a revolt. I'll leave his card on the kitchen table."

He kissed her bare shoulder. "Enjoy your shower."

She smiled, turning her head to look up at him. "I will. Sure you don't want to join me?"

He grinned, cupping her cheek to pull her into a kiss. "Darling, if I join you, I'm not going to get anything done."

"And that would be bad?" she asked teasingly.

He laughed before climbing out of the bed. "Yes, sweetheart, that would be bad."

She propped her head on her hand to better enjoy the view of Liam sliding on his jeans after giving up on finding his underwear. He shot her a quick wink before pulling on his shirt and climbing up the ladder. When he was gone, she curled up into a ball, smiling like a loon before muffling a squeal into her pillow.

Chapter Fifteen: A Very Important Date

"So," Leah said carefully, staring out the windshield at the restaurant, "this is it."

"Yeah." Liam nodded slowly, eyes glued to the entrance. He chewed briefly on his thumbnail before catching her look. Releasing his nail, he studied his thumb as if surprised he'd been doing it. "I thought I had kicked that habit," he murmured.

Leah waited until she couldn't take the silence any longer. "You ready to go in?"

"Nope," he said, sighing before exiting the car. After opening her door, he held out his hand to assist her, brows furrowing as his gaze immediately drifted back to the entrance.

"It's going to be fine," she said, squeezing his hand.

He took a deep breath before nodding and offering her his bent arm.

Taking it, she walked with him into the restaurant. The hostess smiled brightly, confirming their names before leading them back to the table.

"Mr. Leery and Mr. Niels arrived just a few moments ago."

When she spotted Dennis Leery at the table, she smiled widely, her earlier worry forgotten. "Dennis, I didn't put two and two together."

Dennis smiled, standing to hug her. "Probably because I swore I'd never come back to Clearwater. And yet, here I am. Leah, I don't think you've met my husband, Sheldon." Sighing dramatically, he added, "The reason I ever returned."

Sheldon stood with a smile, reaching out to shake Leah's hand. "Pleasure to meet you. I didn't realize you two knew each other."

As they took their seats, Liam didn't bother to hide his grin. "I didn't realize he was that Dennis."

Leah blushed, rolling her eyes and shoving his shoulder lightly.

Sheldon raised an eyebrow. "Something I should know about?"

Leah bit her lip lightly before she answered, "Just some highlights of a youth that were decidedly not misspent."

Dennis grinned. "Some highlights that probably shouldn't be shared at the dinner table."

Leah covered her mouth to hide her grin, but her eyes danced with humor. "And that," she agreed.

"Color me intrigued," Sheldon murmured.

Dennis hummed, sitting back in his chair. "I might satisfy your intrigue, provided I obtain the appropriate permission, of course."

Leah laughed and waved a hand. "By all means. If you can keep some secrets, Mr. Niels."

"Please, call me Sheldon."

She smiled, relieved to have that social nicety out of the way. "Only if you call me Leah."

He tipped an imaginary hat. "Will do. As for your question, yes, I can keep a secret. But I'm not so sure I want to know."

"We had some questions that we answered through experimentation,"

Leah offered carefully. "Some outcomes were worse than others."

Dennis laughed, shoulders shaking lightly with his amusement. When he recovered, he squeezed his husband's shoulder. "I promise not to share anything you wouldn't want to hear."

Sheldon turned to Liam, arching a single eyebrow. "I take it you've heard these stories?"

Liam shook his head ruefully. "Some of them. I was dragged into a couple of them. I'm sure there are more I'll never hear."

Leah smiled innocently when Sheldon turned his gaze to her. "Some things just aren't meant to be shared."

"Mature point of view for how young you must have been. Dennis left town right after graduation, right?"

"You know," Dennis mused, "I'm not sure if it was a measure of maturity, a lack of incentive to share, the fun of keeping secrets, fear of getting caught, or some combination of all of the above, but we can certainly call it maturity."

Leah grinned. "Yes," she agreed, pointing to Dennis, "that. Potentially also the avoiding the law aspect played into it."

Dennis snorted and tipped his glass toward her in agreement. "That may have had a little something to do with it."

Sheldon's eyebrows climbed, and Leah cast him a reassuring smile. "We were young and dumb and didn't think some things all of the way through. We were a little too into mayhem and pranks." She cast a glance at Liam, seeing his lips twitching as he fought a smile. She cleared her throat. "Anyway, I think we made it all of the way through our reparations list before Dennis fled the city."

She turned to Dennis, "How *did* you end up back in Clearwater?"

Dennis grinned, accepting the change of subject gracefully. "Sheldon and I met in grad school. He was offered department head with not only the approval to pursue his passion project but actual excitement. He'd been talking about pursuing experiential learning in journalism more, and the local paper here was intrigued.

"Fortunately for his dreams, the high school happened to be looking for a drama teacher at the same time. It was the best set of jobs we could find, and Sheldon promised to move after a year, if it was as awful as I was expecting."

He rolled his eyes before casting his husband a fond smile. "I've come to appreciate Clearwater's charms more over the years, and it didn't hurt that I was able to start a collaboration between the college theater department and the high school's." He frowned, eyebrows furrowing.

"What's wrong?" Leah asked, concern churning her stomach.

Dennis cleared his throat before offering her a grim smile. "The tornado took out the auditorium we planned to use for the production. I just found out before we came that they're not planning to rebuild.

"Hell, even if they were going to rebuild, it wouldn't be done in time for the play. The summer theater kids have been working hard this year on a Snow White retelling. Sucks to have to disappoint them like this."

Liam frowned. "Can't you use the gym at the school?"

Dennis shook his head. "It's closed for repairs for the summer, and a lot of the cast will be elsewhere once it's reopened. Can't wait for the school year reopening to have it. Sorry, I didn't mean to bring the mood down. Some of the kids were going to use this production for their portfolios."

"That's awful," Leah said. "How much space do you need for the play?"

"You remember how big the school's gym is?"

Leah cocked her head, picturing the space in her head before nodding.

"The space in the gym would've been a bit tight but decent. Why do you ask? Any leads I can take shameless advantage of?"

"I'd have to take a closer look at it, but we're in the process of clearing out the arena to show off the space. I think it'd be big enough. You'd need a stage and seating, but it might be a decent short-notice substitute."

"Seriously?" Dennis asked, leaning forward.

"Whoa, don't get too excited. It would still need a lot of work to get everything clean, and someone should look it over to make sure it's still sound."

Liam gave her a sideways glance. "The barn is sound."

She rolled her eyes. "Still, I'd prefer it be looked over before we push a bunch of people, particularly kids, into it. You can come over and look at it, if you want."

"I do want. Tomorrow morning?"

She narrowed her eyes playfully. "How early are you thinking?"

He laughed, holding up his hands. "No earlier than eight, I promise"

She sighed, shaking her head with faux pain. "I suppose I can give up some of my sleep for you." They shared a grin, each remembering different early-morning shenanigans.

The rest of the dinner passed smoothly. Although Sheldon didn't say it outright, it was looking good for Liam to be back on his former footing with the tenure committee. He held a lot of sway over the final decision, and Liam had worried about his opinion on a personal level.

Burrowing under her covers that night, she smiled, remembering the soft kiss and sincere thank you Liam had given her after dropping her off.

Leah met Dennis at the pasture fence with a smile, mood brightening at his broad grin. His gaze was fixed on the large barn behind her. The sight of him bouncing lightly, eyes shining like a kid on Christmas morning, made her laugh softly.

She turned, leaning back against the fence to take in the barn with fresh eyes. It was an impressive sight. Painted the traditional red with white accents, it loomed large near the edge of the trees. Sadie's husband had wooed her with the massive structure sporting an indoor riding arena, spacious tack room, airy office, and stalls that could open directly into the pasture.

As a teen, Leah had dreamed of turning some of the space into a wedding venue. Sadie had loved the idea, sharing the dream to bring life, love, and laughter back into the space. A fresh wave of grief washed over her. She'd do just about anything to be able to realize their dreams together. Shaking herself out of the melancholy thoughts, she turned back to Dennis.

"I don't know about the inside, obviously, but this looks perfect."

"I thought you'd like it. Just remember," she warned, "the arena hasn't been dealt with in a while. You can see the floor for sure, but the stacks are... impressive."

He nodded slowly. "Consider me forewarned. Just know, all of the hopes and dreams of this year's theater group are riding on your accurate representation of the space."

She groaned dramatically. "Please tell me you didn't tell them already."

He shrugged, spreading his arms wide. "What was I supposed to do? The club president called me last night crying because she just found out they aren't going to rebuild the theater, and *this can't be the theater group legacy she leaves behind*. I had to calm her down somehow."

"I see you've gotten real good at those boundaries, Mr. Leery."

"Hey, little Miss Pot over there. You going to tell me your law job doesn't drain every last bit of energy you have? At least I get some of that energy back."

She stuck her tongue out at him rather than answer. Ducking under the fence, she gestured for him to follow, leading him to the side entrance of the barn.

He chuckled before climbing over the fence to follow. "You've done a lot to clean it up."

She nodded and shot him a quick grin. "Thanks for noticing. The little war Liam started, and ended, turned out to be a blessing. As much as I don't love to admit it, this part of the barn wouldn't be anywhere near usable at this point without him. I'm looking forward to showing it off to the next group of potential partners and investors."

"I heard you had another meeting coming up." When she raised an eyebrow, he shrugged.

"I'm tight with Ros, woman. Not much gets past our combined network of sources. I suggested she put a bee in your bonnet about some straight-up fundraising, but she rightly told me that adding fundraising to your plate would be a less-than-ideal path toward success."

She grinned, bumping his shoulder as they walked. "Thanks, Leery."

He returned the grin before checking her shoulder in return. "Sure thing, Carter."

"I'm going to host the investors' meeting in the barn, so I don't need to worry about the weather. That third weekend in August always seems to have something."

He laughed. "Don't I know it." When his stride slowed, she looked over to catch his frown. "It's the third weekend in August?"

"Yeah, why?"

He rolled his eyes. "It's not a big deal. We usually have the play that third weekend, but we can move it to whichever weekend works for you."

She nodded before pulling open the side door, leading him down the aisle toward the arena doors. "If we have people come in this way, they'll need to walk by the office. It shares a wall that is mostly window with the arena, and we can use it to take tickets, maybe sell some concessions."

When they passed the tack room and aforementioned office, she opened the large doors into the arena. The space was filled with stacked boxes, piles of wood, water softener salt, old wheelbarrows, and other odds and ends. The boxes she'd removed, plus the absence of Liam's car, had cleared up some of the floor space. It made the remaining piles *slightly* less daunting.

"I see what you mean about it needing to be cleaned out," Dennis said slowly, making his way between the stacks.

"Yeah," Leah agreed with a sigh before following him. "This was next on the list. Most of the boxes can be taken into town to be donated. Liam sent off a video of most of the contents to my cousins last week. The boxes stacked on that end," she pointed to the plastic totes stacked neatly against the far wall, "all need to be kept and should fit in the tack room.

"We should be able to squeeze in the rest of what needs to be kept, with any overflow fitting in one or two of the unused stalls, which will leave the office for anything you need to store. I was thinking we could put up some temporary walls on that side to act as a backstage and changing area." She shrugged. "But you're the expert, so you tell me."

Reaching the center of the room, he slowly spun around in a circle, taking it all in. "Yes," he said, voice soft as he thought. "I think it would work. I need to talk to Sam about a stage. Putting up some large curtains and temporary rooms should definitely work for backstage and changing areas."

Looking at the boxes and other haphazardly organized piles, he grinned. "The theater kids could get this cleaned up in no time. You'd need to be here, of course, to direct where it all goes. If we get it cleaned out this week, we won't even be behind in rehearsals."

He bounced again, eyes dancing. "Do you have the time?"

His excitement filled her with warmth. "Yeah, I do. Do you really think they'd be willing to help with the clean out? Liam has been tackling it for me."

"In exchange for a stage? Absolutely, and they'll probably love you for it."

He continued to look around, his smile growing. "Yes, this will work. Did you have anything in mind for seating?"

"About that," she said, the last pieces of an idea clicking into place. "What do you think about doing dinner and a show? Combine the shrimp boil with the play in a way. Dinner first, and then the play. I can move the pitch to be before the actual dinner, and the people wanting to see the play can also get a ticket to the shrimp boil."

She shrugged, not sure if he was excited or horrified. "It's already going to be a big undertaking, so making more of the shrimp boil shouldn't make it that much worse. Plus, then you could charge for the dinner tickets and raise some money for a new stage."

He studied her in silence for several long beats before nodding. "I like it. Only problem will be next year when they don't get the food option."

She smiled, relieved he wasn't dismissing the idea as an overreach.

Dennis's eyes flicked around the space, clearly thinking through the logistics. When he spoke again, he sounded like he was thinking out loud rather than speaking to her. "The older kids will for sure help with serving and setup, maybe even cooking. Some of them can be trusted to do the serving in costume, but I should probably have backup costumes available just in case."

Excitement coursed through her as she caught up with his thought process. The theater kids helping with the shrimp boil would take so much off her plate, leaving her more breathing room to impress Ros's investors. And, a quiet part of her piped up, giving her more time to work on that piece. The time Liam had bullied her into taking had gotten her farther than she anticipated being possible.

"Should the profits from the shrimp boil tickets go to the theater department or the kids directly, do you think?" she asked, bringing her mind back to the logistics.

Dennis raised an eyebrow. Waving in the direction of the would-be stage, he said, "Dude. Stage. You are providing your local thespians with a place to put on a play that otherwise would have had to be canceled. You keep the proceeds."

Before she could protest, he waved his hand around. "This is what I meant by doing some fundraising for the farm. Without you being here, no stage, maybe for a long time."

She bit her lip, hoping her eyes weren't obviously watery.

He smiled gently. "We want you here as much as you want to be here."

Then, like the A+ friend he was, he added a dramatic flair to his voice. "Besides being a goddess among men for providing them a stage, every single one of them wants this farm to stay here, not to see it replaced by some large corporate whatever. You're dealing with thespians, girlie. Theater nerds are the best crew to have on your side."

Chapter Sixteen: A More Private Picnic

After Liam stepped out of his car, she tangled their hands together and pulled him in for a quick kiss. Her good intentions were shot to hell as soon as their lips met, and she sank into the kiss with a happy sigh. She leaned her body flush against his before releasing his hands to stick hers in his back pockets, copping a feel while trying to pull him impossibly closer. Pulling back minutely, she felt his lips curl into a smile against hers. Palms bracketing her hips, his thumbs dipped beneath her waistband.

She shivered lightly, pulling back enough to look up into his eyes. Her heart melted at his soft expression. Voice breathy, she asked, "Good day?"

"Better now," he answered, eyes twinkling with pleasure and amusement. "Yours?"

"Fantastic, and yet, somehow even better now."

Recalling her earlier plan, she gave him a quick peck on the lips before recapturing his hand to tow him to the pile of blankets she had set up behind the barn. He allowed himself to be pulled, smiling gamely. As they walked toward the blankets, she filled him in on her meeting with Dennis.

Sam would be over early the next morning to assess the logistics of setting up a stage. Provided they got final approval from Sam, they would direct more energy to cleaning out the barn with the assistance of the theater cast and crew. After Dennis left, Leah had spent the rest of the day double-checking boxes, taking photos to send to her cousins, and moving the rest of the stuff into piles to donate, throw away, or store after their responses. The toss and donate piles were significantly higher than the store pile.

"So, yeah, good day," she said, warmth suffusing her when he gave her another fond smile. "Did you get what you needed done?"

"I survived the final round of interviews. I think they went okay?" He waffled his hand back and forth. "Hard to say for sure, but they seemed promising. In between the interviews, I finished the syllabi for next semester. The posts about your shrimp boil are up with some more scheduled. I'll tweak them to add in the play once that's confirmed. Dinner and a show is a great idea."

She blushed at the compliment, melting into him when he freed his hand to draw his arm around her.

He pulled her into a soft kiss when they reached the nest of blankets she'd set up near the side of the barn. "Definitely better now," he said softly.

She bit her lip, wondering briefly if her next question would ruin the mood. "How'd your meeting with Sheldon go?"

Liam sighed, running his free hand through his hair. "He seemed to be giving me hints that it was pretty much in the bag. Just need to keep them happy through the cocktail hours coming up, and I might actually get tenure." His expression warred between worry and elation.

She frowned, rubbing her hand up and down his arm. "I'm sorry you have to wait so long to get an answer."

"Thanks. Bright side. He loves you and thinks you're the best thing that could've happened to me. Called you forgiving me an absolute miracle."

She pulled back with a grin, laughter dancing in her eyes. "A miracle, you say? Does that mean you're going to finish setting up the projector while I cocoon in the blankets?"

Laughing loudly, he pulled her back into a hug, kissing the top of her head when she snuggled into his chest. "I will never understand how you can be comfortable buried under a thousand blankets when it's this warm out."

She looked up at him, propping her chin against his chest. "So, yes?"

He squeezed her tightly before kissing her on the forehead. "So, yes, dear. I'll go finish setting up the projector, so your freakish self can start the overheating process."

"Mmmm," she murmured, "excellent." When he released her, she promptly dropped to the blanket pile, burrowing in until the blankets were arranged to her satisfaction.

She smiled as she watched him walk to the ancient projector, enjoying the sight of his ass in his formfitting jeans and the way his broad shoulders filled out his shirt.

He stopped several feet away, looking back over his shoulder and raising an eyebrow at her. "Are you objectifying me, sweetheart?"

She leaned back, supporting herself on her hands. "Maybe," she said, drawing out the word.

He cracked a grin and started to walk backwards. "Well, if it's only maybe..."

She laughed, allowing her head to fall back and shaking her loose hair out so it cascaded almost to the ground, knowing he'd enjoy both the flash of cleavage the position would create and the sight of her hair unbound. When she looked back, he had stopped walking, and she caught a brief flash of tongue wetting his lips.

Biting her bottom lip, she straightened again and smiled. "If your ego really needs the boost, then, yes, darling, I'd say it's safe to say I'm frequently objectifying you. Are you objectifying me?"

He flicked his eyes up and down her figure once more, a slow grin spreading across his lips. "If I weren't before, I certainly am now, darlin'."

She grinned and twirled her finger in a circle. "Well, then you better get that projector set up, so we can actually do something about it."

He snapped a quick, casual salute before spinning around. "Yes, ma'am."

She bit her lip again, enjoying the slow burn of arousal. Her mind oh so helpfully reminded her of past nights they'd spent together. Except now, they were adults, and every touch burned so much hotter.

Liam made quick work of turning on the projector, repositioning it so the movie filled the white fabric stretched across the barn wall, and starting the movie. Leah smiled softly at the sight of the opening credits of *The Wizard of Oz* playing across the barn. It had been a favorite of hers as a teen. Liam had driven her over three hours one way to watch the movie at a drive-in theater. It was one of the few periods of real peace they had shared as teens.

Her parents had been on a river cruise, so they weren't constantly checking in and complaining about her relationship. Liam's father had been serving a short stretch in jail, and his mom had taken Liam's siblings to visit her parents. At the time, Leah had worried his mother wouldn't return, leaving Liam alone with his father. In hindsight, it probably would've been better for everyone involved if she had used the opportunity. She shook herself out of the maudlin thoughts, choosing to remember the feel of his hand in hers as they drove back that night.

Returning to her side, he settled himself behind her, pulling her toward him until her back rested solidly against his chest. He draped his arms around her body, clasping his wrist with his opposite hand over her blanket-covered stomach. She hummed with pleasure, feeling perfectly cozy within the tangle of blankets and Liam.

As the movie played, he dropped slow kisses against the side of her neck and the top of her shoulders, darting his tongue out to taste her skin. Pushing his hands underneath the covers, he dragged his fingers up and down her arms before dipping beneath her shirt to stroke up and down her ribs.

Over time, his hands skated to her stomach. Long strokes stopped just beneath her breasts before making their achingly slow way back down to the waistband of her skirt. Heat pooled in her core as his fingers danced inches away from where she wanted them. She pushed back against him with a moan and clasped her hands over his.

She shuddered when he scraped his teeth lightly along her neck to the edge of her shoulder. He placed a trail of feather-light kisses along the same path his teeth traveled, darting his tongue out in a pattern she couldn't predict. Her hands clenched around his as he hit every erogenous zone she had in between. Chills raced up and down her spine as her core begged for more attention.

Leaning back into him, she drew her knees up to rest on either side of his, spreading herself open. He traced his tongue up her neck, placing an open-mouth kiss behind her ear before he nipped her earlobe.

"As you please, sweetheart," he murmured, arousal thick in his voice.

He pulled his hands out from under her shirt, leaving her momentarily cold. He blazed a new path of heat as he skated his strong hands down her thighs until he reached bare skin beneath the hem of her skirt. Slowly, so fucking slowly, he drew the hem up over her knees and down her thighs to rest at her waist. His calloused fingers traced up and down her thigh beneath the blanket, sending sparks straight to her core. She arched up with a moan, dropping her head back on his shoulder to stare up at the stars.

"Heightens touch, right?" he asked, voice coated with arousal and a dash of humor.

Years ago, he had complained about the lack of view when they had indulged themselves on a cool night. As a teen, she'd had a habit of hiding insecurities with bravado, so she'd tartly informed him that his lack of sight heightened his sense of touch. Although they both knew her point made little sense, he had ultimately gone down on her underneath the blankets until she was a twitching and overheated mess. She'd ultimately tossed the blankets off herself, so it had worked out splendidly for the both of them.

"Yes, exactly." Her soft laugh turned into a breathy moan when his fingers traced her waistband, dipping closer to her core.

The torturously slow slide of his fingers up and down her thighs kept her firmly rooted in the present. Each slow stroke up brought him closer to her hips, closer to discovering she had nothing on beneath her skirt.

"My, my, Miss Carter," he purred when his fingers skated up over her hips and underneath the band of her skirt from below. "How beautifully naughty of you."

His palms rested against her hips, the tips of his fingers playing near the edge of her pubic mound, while his thumbs moved in a slow arch along her lower belly.

"Fuck, please," she panted, arching back further.

He dragged his teeth along her neck, pressing down where it met her shoulder. She shuddered beneath his hands, trembling as he sucked lightly against the spot. Pulling back, he blew against the wet spot, making her moan and arch again.

His cock dug into the small of her back with the new position. He cursed, hips twitching against her. *Fuck,* she needed to hold on to something. She braced her hands under his bent knees, moving them mindlessly up and down his thighs.

Finally, finally, he moved his hands from her hips to play closer to her center. He pulled her thighs farther apart before sliding his hands down to rest at the apex of each thigh. His thumbs slowly traced along her mound, sending sparks of delicious sensation. Her head lolled against his shoulder while she panted, chest heaving.

The blankets slid down her front, but she ignored it. She was warm enough; they were generating enough heat. But he stopped. She groaned, digging her hands into him. He kissed her neck with a mumbled apology but didn't move his fingers.

Craning her neck to look back at him, she couldn't help but giggle. His eyes flicked to hers before returning to the newly bared cleavage, a wry grin spreading across his face. Her squirming had pushed the shirt down farther, baring the top of her bra.

"Yeah," he said slowly, "that's going to need to come off."

She bit her lip, contemplating. Sure, she was warm enough *now*. She arched with a gasp, hands spasming against his large thighs, when he unexpectedly dragged his fingers down her folds. She relaxed back against him with a shudder when he stopped.

She blinked into the night, dazed. A second ago, she would have said she wasn't so worked up that his request would be anywhere close to convincing. Fuck it. They'd be warm enough. She elbowed him. "Yours too."

When he laughed, she twisted around to stick her tongue out before batting her eyes at him innocently. "I need the extra heat, darling. You don't want me to be cold, do you?"

"Can't have that," he agreed, voice raspy.

He kept one hand on her while reaching back with the other to pull his shirt off. Her mouth watered at the ripple of his toned abdomen and the newly bared flesh. She grinned at his expression. He deserved the cocky grin.

Turning back around, she grabbed the hem of her shirt with both hands before pulling it up and off. She shivered lightly in the cool air but found herself nestled back into his hot chest in short order. The lacy bra she wore didn't provide much coverage, but the boost to her girls was worth it.

Her breasts danced with the shudder that went through her when he replaced his other hand and resumed his ministrations. If she weren't already spiraling higher into arousal, she would have laughed. Clever man.

His hands mirrored each other as they finally parted her folds. One long finger dragged up and down either side, again and again. She whimpered, moving her head back and forth against his shoulder. The slow drag was maddening, making her writhe against him.

She cried out, arching back when he dipped two fingers into her while another circled her clit. Waves of pleasure cascaded through her, sending a rush down to the tips of her fingers and toes before crashing back into her core.

He added a third finger, fucking into her slowly as she panted. His breathing was controlled, an easy breath in and out as he played her like an instrument. Heat from his breath washed across her chest, drawing her nipples even tighter.

"Liam, *please*," she moaned.

A lightning bolt of pleasure crashed through her when he crooked his fingers against her G-spot while applying light pressure to her clit. Her hips jerked as her core spasmed around his fingers. He continued fucking his fingers in and out, circling her most sensitive spots, to draw out her pleasure. She melted against him, stars sparking across her vision.

She blinked dazedly, slowly pulling back her ability to think and move as he traced his damp fingers along her hip and upper thigh. She lay in his arms for long moments, muscles spasming as she pulled herself back together.

Slowly, she drew her legs back together, pausing when her core spasmed again with the movement. She twisted to face him, and he drew her into a heated kiss. His eyes danced when they pulled apart.

Her eyes flicked down, pausing briefly at the bulge in his slacks before returning her gaze to his with a smirk. "We should take care of that."

He laughed before shucking his pants off, pulling a condom out and rolling it on. She braced herself against the ground, still a little wobbly. He earned the smirk crawling across his face, she thought wryly.

She knelt to face him, pushing off her skirt before pulling him into a kiss. She moved forward to straddle his thighs, making an appreciative noise when he cupped her ass to draw her forward. Wrapping her fingers around his cock, she traced up and down the length before using her hold to guide him into her. He broke the kiss, panting as he rested his forehead against hers. They both looked down, watching as she slid down his length.

Taking him to the hilt in a single wet slide, she shuddered at the pleasantly full feeling. The harsh breaths he'd taken during her slow slide down did wonders for her own ego.

She set a slow pace, sparks immediately dancing along her spine. Reaching behind her, he unsnapped her bra, swallowing harshly when her breasts sprang free. He caught a nipple, sucking it into his mouth when she moved up. Shuddering, she stilled against him as he sucked. She sank her hands into his hair while his tongue swirled along her tight bud.

The cool air against her wet nipple made her shiver when he released her. Her quick drop down his cock made her shudder for a different reason. Eyes darkening, he tipped her over onto her back. His arms and the pile of blankets beneath her cushioned the drop. He braced himself above her, holding her gaze as he pounded into her. As she tipped her head back, her mouth dropped open, and her hands fisted the blankets beneath her.

He'd clearly remembered the angle from last night. The fast pace that was making her see stars already was all him. The thought that they wouldn't last long had barely crossed her mind before she was spasming around his cock, pulling him over the edge with her.

Chapter Seventeen: Here Comes the Rain

Leah's ringtone jerked her out of a nightmare featuring snakes in the shrimp boil. A shiver of revulsion coursed through her before she glanced at her phone screen long enough to see it was Derek. "What's up?" she asked, voice rough with sleep.

"Hey, Lee. I'm sorry to do this to you last minute, but I'm not going to be able to make it out to your show or the pregame."

She rubbed the sleep out of her eyes, mind already whirring with the worst-case scenarios. Derek dropped out well in advance, not at the last minute. "That's fine. What's going on? Are you okay?"

He sighed heavily. "I'm fine. My company's asshole in-house counsel got it into her head that now would be the best time to fire Smith. He had four site inspections scheduled for today. Of fucking course all of them need to happen today, or the projects are going to be delayed. Which wouldn't be a big deal, if he hadn't been screwing around already. They're already overdue."

"Shit, Derek. I'm sorry; that sounds awful."

He sighed again, his frustration clear. "It'll be fine. Everything is on fire. This month is going to be hell. But it's fine."

She grimaced at the familiar refrain. "So, coming to the shrimp boil isn't looking good either?"

"Fucking hell," he groaned.

Through the line, she heard what sounded like the scrape of a table across the floor, followed in close succession by a crash, the sound of glass breaking, and a stream of expletives. "What—what did I do to deserve this?! Fucking hell."

She winced. He was more stressed than he was willing to admit. He usually would have at least covered the phone in deference to her gender, something she had given up on arguing with him about. "You okay, Der?"

"Yeah, I just bumped the table. I can't believe I forgot about the shrimp boil. Yes, I'm probably going to need to miss it. Paige will still be able to make it, though, right?" His voice was ragged, making her clench heart with worry.

She hesitated, wanting to tell him that Paige would be there to take some of the stress off his plate but ultimately unwilling to lie to him. "No, she's got some stuff going on that she needs to deal with. But, hey, no need to worry. Dennis and I have nailed down the logistics for how we're going to handle everything.

"The theater kids are stoked to serve in costume, and Ros's potential investors are excited about the show. Most of our thespians are planning to stay in character while serving, which should be highly entertaining. Between Dennis, the theater group, and Liam, we should have it more than handled. It's covered, I promise."

"Are you sure? Really sure, not just trying to stop me from worrying?"

"I'm positive," she said firmly. "It's going to work out, Derek. The show really isn't a big deal. Let me know if I can do anything for you. Is the firing something he wants to fight?"

Derek laughed without humor. "I'm sure he does, but from what it sounds like, he was getting up to something on company time that he shouldn't have been. He was an asshole and, frankly, not that great at his job, but if she had waited literally one more week, it wouldn't have been as much of a shit storm."

"Shit, Derek. I'm really sorry. Lawyers suck."

He laughed. "Well, this one certainly does. I'm kind of fond of you, though."

"I wish I could do something to help."

"Lady, no," he groaned. "You have too much on your plate already. I am the one wishing he could do more. And, seriously? What's this about the show not being a big deal? Of course your show is a big deal. It's huge."

She blushed. "Thanks, Derek. Good luck today. Let me know if I can do anything. Happy to listen if you need an ear."

"Thanks, Lee. I might take you up on that. Ditto on the good luck."

Pulling out her phone, she texted Liam to let him know about the change in plans, smiling when his response came back immediately.

> You've got this, sweetheart. I'm on track to wrap up early this afternoon. I'll see you as soon as I'm done but no later than three.

> Perfect. See you then.

Leah scowled at her phone. 3:15 stared back, mocking her. She rolled her eyes before propelling herself out of the desk chair to pace up and down the short hall in front of the door. If she was going to make it to the gallery on time, she needed to leave soon. Without her boyfriend. Who was missing without a word. Again.

She let out a deep breath, closing her eyes. She hit her phone against her thigh twice before looking at the screen again. The lack of a message alert was also mocking her. She was not going to restart it again. And she absolutely was not going to call Liam again. She'd feel like a stalker or a crazy girlfriend. But, if he were hurt, not calling him would be bad. Except, she had called him three times already.

Oh, fuck it. It rang twice before she was sent to his voicemail. She hung up. She'd already left a message.

> Is everything okay?

> Can you text me when you're on the way?

> Or just let me know you're okay?

> Please.

Before she could decide on her next move, her phone vibrated in her hand. Cassidy's name was not the one she hoped to see.

> GIIIRRRRRRLLLLLL!!!!! You must be on the way to the show now. Woot woot!!!

> You're going to kill it!!!!!

> It's going to be awesome, Lee. Wish I was there!

> Same here!! Thanks for the virtual hype, doll. :-)

> I hope it will be.

It will!

Regardless, you did the thing! You're in a show!

Want to talk, or is Liam keeping you sufficiently distracted? Derek told me he and Paige weren't able to make it down.

> Yeah, things blew up at work for both of them.

Leah waited, considering what to tell her about Liam.

Should I take that as a yes, Liam is keeping you sufficiently distracted? *laughing face emoji*

> About that.
>
> Do you still have Alec's phone number?

I think so, why?

> Liam isn't here, and he's not answering my calls or texts. I'm worried something's happened to him.

Yeah, I'll text him, let you know what he says.

> Thanks, boo.

> No prob. I think you need to head out now, though. Let him catch up. You don't want to be late for the show.

> What if he's hurt?

After casting one more glance out the window toward the driveway to find no one coming, Leah returned to the bathroom to finish getting ready. He was just running late, and his phone died. She needed to be ready to leave as soon as he got here, or she was going to be late.

When her phone vibrated against the bathroom counter, she pulled it out quickly, mentally crossing her fingers for a text from Liam.

> Unknown Number: Liam is fine. Not going to be playing chauffeur for your little show tonight, though, so you're going to have to do something for yourself for once.

A stab of guilt hit her. Maybe she had pushed him too far. Asked for too much. She closed her eyes, leaning forward against the counter. No. She wasn't letting Alec get to her. They were helping each other. And she might have been tempted to push further, but she hadn't asked for anything unnecessary. Whatever she may have done wrong, she had to get herself to that show. They would figure the rest out later.

Leah stared at her steering wheel, numb with shock. "What the ever-loving fuck?" There was no way this was happening.

She took a deep breath, shaking her head to clear it. She was overreacting. Her car was just a little cranky from sitting for a while. The engine was going to turn over on the second try. Because the universe was not this much of an asshole.

She chose to ignore the obvious trembling in her hand when she turned the key in the ignition. Nothing. No whine, no attempts to turn over the engine. Dread pooled in her stomach. Deep breathing made her feel like she was going to start hyperventilating. Normal breathing. *It's fine. Everything is fine.*

She pushed herself back against the seat, trying to focus on her breaths. Why couldn't something be easy for once? One obstacle was more than sufficient. This was just excessive.

"Okay, Lee. No one is coming to save you. What are you going to do to help yourself?"

Her mind spun too fucking slowly for several long moments. Sam, she thought, hope surging. He would be close by on deliveries. It had to be the battery. She had just had the alternator replaced. A quick jump, and she'd be on her way.

Her hand still shook as she pulled out her phone to call for help. After the last several calls she had made, she half expected the sound of Sam's voicemail picking up. When he answered, her throat felt tight.

"Lee, are you okay? What's going on?"

The worry in his voice almost made it worse, but she managed to rasp out a quick assurance.

"Yeah, you don't sound that fine. Where are you?"

"Sadie's," Leah forced out.

"Alright, I'm a minute out. I'll be there soon."

Leah nodded, barely registering that he couldn't see her before they hung up. Her head fell forward against the steering wheel. Watching the tears roll down the fake leather of the wheel was oddly soothing. The thought that she was probably ruining her makeup floated through her mind but was gone as easily as it came.

The sound of Sam at her car door made her jump. He was staring at her.

He was saying something, expression worried. What was he saying? She blinked, and the door was open. His form went in and out of focus as a rushing sound filled her ears.

She barely felt it as he unbuckled her seat belt before gently urging her out of the car and into the house. The next thing that truly registered was setting down an empty glass. They were at the kitchen table. She shook her head. This time, he came into focus easily.

"Better now?" he asked, voice calm.

She nodded, rubbing her hands over her face. "I'm so sorry about that," she said, voice rough. "That hasn't happened since college."

He shook his head and shrugged. "Nothing to be sorry about."

He grabbed her glass to refill it, moving to the fridge. "Shouldn't you be on your way to your show?"

She was grateful he had turned away from her, or the waterworks would've started again. Instead, she took a shuddery breath and told him her car wouldn't start.

He caught her gaze when he set the glass down. "I'll go take a look. Stay here. Take a minute."

She nodded. "Thank you. Thank you so much."

He nodded and shot her a quick grin. "What're friends for?"

As she drank the water, she felt soothed by the noises coming from outside. His truck starting up and pulling closer to her car. The hoods being propped open. On her way to the bathroom to wash her face, panic rushed through her. His clothes. *Fuck*. He and his partner were going on a trip today. They were supposed to leave shortly after she and Liam had planned to leave.

"Shit," she muttered as her eyes fell on Sadie's wall clock. She ran out the door in time to see him starting her own car. The fear she had ruined his vacation eclipsed her elation at the running car.

His brows furrowed. "Now what's happening?"

"You need to go."

"Ah, gratitude, so nice. That's one of the things I love most about you, Lee. Your genuine, heart-touching expressions of gratitude."

She flapped her hands in frustration. "Jason is going to kill me if you don't leave right now."

He snorted as he pulled out his phone. "I have plenty of time." Glancing down, he blanched. "Oh shit, I have to go." He quickly removed the cables from the batteries and jogged to his truck. "Don't turn it off again until it's been running at least twenty minutes, and don't forget to wash your face!"

As he pulled out in a cloud of dust, she screamed her "thank you" after him. Fishing her phone out of her car's cupholder, she shot off a quick text to Jason.

> I'm so sorry!!!! He's on his way. Have I wrecked your vacation?

Her heart sank at his crying face emoji followed by the "Everything is on fire" GIF. Fortunately for her heart, the messages were quickly followed by a laughing face emoji.

> We're good. This vacation is happening, and we are going to have a fabulous time.

> Thanks for the heart attack.

> Welp, you started it.

> You have so little faith in me, you think I don't know him well enough by now to build in ALL the extra time.

> That's… fair. I'm sorry I thought so little of you.

> Have a great time!

> You too. Get on the road, woman!

Chapter Eighteen: Lights, Camera, Action

"Hey, Mads," Leah said when Madison answered her call. Her voice was admirably steady.

"What's wrong?" Okay, apparently her voice wasn't *that* steady.

Madison's concern caused tears to well. She took a deep breath before trying to speak again. "I was wondering if I could stop by your place to clean up. I'm running late, but I really need to clean up before I get to the gallery."

"Absolutely. How much of a cleanup are we talking?"

The tears cleared up; she had a plan. It would all be fine. "Just my face. Unless you have a cure for panic attacks. I could use that too. I think my hair is fine, but my face is a mess."

"Okay, here's the plan. The gallery is too far from my place, I think. I'll grab my kit, we'll get you cleaned up in your car, or in the bathroom of The Bar. It's right across from the gallery, and I can get us in the back no problem."

"Okay." That was better. Madison had the best plans. And Leah was good at following them. Most of the time.

"Okay," Madison agreed, voice warm. "I'll meet you there. Drive safe."

"Thanks, love," Leah said, voice thick.

"Anytime, hun. I'll see you in about twenty?"

The surprise chased away the last of her tears. She laughed softly. Of course. She'd shared her location with Madison when they both got lost one too many times at the last company retreat.

"Remembering my stalkery ways?" Madison asked, voice teasing.

"Feeling very grateful for your stalkery ways," she corrected, smile growing.

Madison squeezed her hand as they walked into the gallery together. Tasha's broad smile and wave was a welcome sight. Leah felt herself unwinding. They'd made it, and Tasha wasn't pissed.

"Wonderful, you made it just in time," Tasha said warmly, skating over the fact that Leah was not, in fact, on time. "The artists are taking a final look at their pieces, and then we'll be open to the public before we know it. Months of prep for an hours-long event." She grinned brightly.

"I've had a few calls about your piece, Leah. I'm so glad you were able to get it finished before the show. Your smaller pieces are lovely, of course, but the big pieces are hot right now. It's really everything your aunt said it would be." She squeezed Leah's arm briefly. "The perfect way to honor her." Tasha gave them both one last warm smile before wandering away to greet her other exhibiting artists.

"She's right, you know. From what you've told me about Sadie, she would be absolutely thrilled with all of this."

Leah bit her lip. With the farm at risk, she wasn't so sure.

"Lee," Madison said patiently, "she would've wanted this for you more than you keeping the farm. I know you love the property, but your job is killing you, possibly literally."

"It's hardly *killing* me," Leah protested. Sure, she didn't love the work, but it was fine. Stable. Reliable. She was helping people.

Madison narrowed her eyes. "I'm serious. I've watched you drag yourself into the office for months. Any sane person would acknowledge that practicing family law takes its toll. This could be your out. The farm is also still a very real possibility, but this is more important."

Leah sighed. She knew Madison had a point, but... "I don't think I'd ever forgive myself if I lose this farm."

Madison's frown deepened, and Leah cast her a small smile.

"I'm fine, Mads. Promise. I'll be fine. I understand your point. Someday, I might even be able to say that you're right. In the meantime, I'm going to go take another look at the setup. Want to snag us some of the good snacks before they're all gone?"

Madison studied her for a beat before nodding. "I'll accept that distraction."

"Thanks, hun."

Madison hugged her quickly before strolling over to the table stuffed with food. She smiled, watching her go, before turning to the area Tasha had pointed out. When it came into view around the bend, she gasped. She'd only ever seen it in the day, without the display lights on it. Tasha's background with lighting design made the piece shine to its best advantage.

Reflection played along the dragon's body, adding to the illusion of flight. Tasha had created a flickering effect against the agate Leah had worked into the flames the dragon was spewing, making the rock dance as if truly aflame. Tasha's eye for design ensured they didn't look out of place, but her smaller pieces were definitely outshone, she thought wryly.

"My God, Leah," Madison breathed.

She turned to take in Madison staring at the dragon. Her eyes were wide, mouth parted slightly. Pride warmed her. She had done that. Even if no one else saw what Madison did, the look on Madison's face alone was worth the hours of work. Looking back at the dragon, warmth suffused her. And a voice that sounded suspiciously like Madison reminded her, the creation of this piece didn't cost her nearly as much stress as the nastier divorce cases.

Maybe, just maybe, this was what she was meant to be doing. As confident as Tasha had been, Leah had refused to believe this could work out for her. She warred with herself between letting this feeling take hold, truly enjoying the night, or quashing her hopes before the crush of reality pulled her under again.

Madison pulled her close into a sideways hug, breaking Leah out of her thoughts. "Enjoy the moment, Lee. Pretend you are without a single care in the world other than making sure you have an absolutely amazing time tonight."

Leah laughed, leaning into the other woman. "Alright, I can play make believe tonight."

"Great," Madison said brightly. "Because I have the snacks and the carbonated apple juice for after you finish chatting up that nice-looking lady who's been eyeing your dragon."

Leah bit her lip, looking back toward the woman in question briefly. Madison cocked her head to the side before she grinned brightly. "You know, that would be a great euphemism. I just can't decide what for yet."

Madison winked in response to Leah's snort. "Go forth and have a pleasant little chat with a potential patron or several, and when it's too much, give me a sign, and I'll rescue you."

Leah took a deep breath, nodding. Madison was right. This was part of what she wanted. If only the butterflies in her stomach would agree and *stop moving*.

"And, once you've finished," Madison gestured to the table, "snacks await."

"Oh, yes, over here," Tasha said, voice bright. "I wanted to be sure to introduce you to Mr. Alderson. He's great."

Tasha was an absolute godsend. Leah had tried to do as Madison instructed, but she had no idea where to go after a conversation with the sweet young woman Madison had pointed out. Tasha had swooped in, assuring her it was part of her duties as the gallery owner. She took Leah around, introducing her to a whirlwind of people, leaving her to have lively conversations before swooping her up again and depositing another artist in her place. Rinse and repeat. Leah was having an absolute blast. Not needing to decide when to cut the conversation off was a blessing.

Tasha pulled her in the direction of a man Leah had spotted admiring the dragon piece earlier that evening. "Mr. Alderson, I'd like you to meet Leah Carter. Leah, this is Mr. Alderson."

He grinned, eyes crinkling at the corners. "Ms. Carter, it's a pleasure to meet you. I was just admiring your work."

"Leah, please, and thank you."

"Will, then."

Leah smiled, never sure of how to respond after exchanging permission for using someone's first name. Fortunately, he had enough social grace for the two of them. He immediately pushed the conversation in the direction of her pieces, setting her at ease. She adored talking about this work.

"Are you open to commissions moving forward, or are you booked already?"

"Oh, that's the dream," she said, blushing. "This is my first show, so I don't have anything scheduled for my next project."

"Lucky me," he said with a smile. "I can be patient, but it's not nearly as fun as immediate gratification." He gave her a roguish wink.

"I don't know," she said, eyes dancing with her laughter, "there's something to be said for the high of the anticipation."

He groaned theatrically. "You sound like my husband."

She laughed brightly. She hadn't gotten the impression that he was available, but it was great to have the assurance. "And you sound like my college roommate."

He raised his eyebrows, sly smile growing. "Oh? Do tell."

Leah blushed. "I didn't mean it like *that*. Although," she added musingly, "it was true in that way also."

Having just taken a sip of his drink, he choked and immediately fell into a coughing fit.

"Oh, shit, I mean shoot!" She cringed. "Sorry, are you okay?"

He waved her away, the coughing dovetailing into laughing until tears formed in his eyes. Finally straightening, he wheezed in a breath before coughing a final time and wiping his tears away. "Lord, woman. I haven't laughed that hard in too long."

"Glad I could be of service, then."

On her drive home that night, Leah lowered the windows and sang at the top of her lungs to her favorite Taylor Swift songs, keeping herself awake and celebrating her first art show. Regardless of the pieces sold, it was an absolute blast.

Exiting her car at the end of the long drive, Leah raised her face to the sky to enjoy the cooling mist. Spreading her hands out, she spun her way across the yard as the mist turned into a downpour, laughing at the thrilling sensation of dancing in the rain. *This*, this was what she wanted to do. Let go of the fear and the anxiety that had driven her this far and simply... be.

Coming to a slow stop, she lifted her face up to the rain, savoring the rare moment of peace. Whatever happened, it was going to be okay. She was going to be okay.

Chapter Nineteen: The Aftershocks

Leah stepped back when Liam's door swung open. Alec. Of course. Memories she'd tried for years to suppress surged to the surface. Seeing her mother with his father. Agreeing to keep it quiet. Alec's life imploding while hers stayed the same from the outside. Somehow, it hadn't come out. Her parents and Alec's father quietly moved away, ostensibly pursuing work opportunities. His parents divorced after graduation, claiming they'd simply grown apart.

He smirked, likely relishing her discomfort. Leaning against the doorjamb, his six-foot frame loomed over her. He raised a single dark eyebrow. "You just don't know when to quit, do you?" he drawled.

Her cheeks flamed. This was already exhausting. "Is Liam available?"

Alec crossed his arms, studying her silently for increasingly uncomfortable seconds. "You know, I should really tell you no. Give you the chance to save a little face here, but I just don't like you enough for that."

Pushing himself off the doorjamb, he moved back enough to allow her to squeeze by him, gesturing broadly into the apartment as he did. "Liam! Your ex-girlfriend is here."

Turning away from Alec, she closed her eyes, trying to convince herself that Alec was just being his typical asshole self. Liam wasn't going to put her through this again, especially not this close to the college dinner.

"Catch you later, princess." Laughing when she flinched, Alec knocked sharply against the door frame before shutting the door behind him.

Leah rubbed her face and dragged her hands back through her hair as she waited. When Liam made his appearance, her lips parted with a silent gasp. His clothes looked like they'd been slept in, and his eyes were bloodshot. "Are you okay?" she asked, voice soft.

He rubbed his eyes with one hand before nodding. "Yeah, Lee," he said roughly. "I'm fine."

She shook her head, scoffing softly to rid herself of the lump trying to close off her throat. "Great. It's fantastic to be at this point with you."

He leaned back against the wall, crossing his arms. "Which point is that, Lee?"

"Why don't you tell me? From where I'm standing, it looks like the lying and hiding shit from me point."

He clicked his tongue. "I'm sorry I didn't make it to the art show that you repeatedly tried to sabotage for yourself. My father was attacked, so I had to go make sure he didn't die. No worries, though. He was his usual charming self by the time I left this morning. I'm so sorry that, for once, I put someone other than you first."

She laughed without humor. "Fuck you, Liam. You could've told me, and you know damn well I would've been there for you."

"I realize you haven't managed to figure this out yet, so I'll speak slowly. I can take care of myself. I've been managing just fine for the last decade and change without you."

"Oh, of course," she said, sarcasm coating her voice. "What was I thinking? You've been doing a bang-up job when it comes to your father. You didn't sabotage your tenure or anything because of his shitty behavior and toxic worldview. No," she held up a finger, "I know. That was all me. Just existing in this town was enough to drive you off the fucking rails."

Liam pushed off the wall with a scoff. He moved into the kitchen, putting more physical distance between them. "I know this is going to be hard for you to hear, Lee, but you need to hear it. I. Don't. Need. You. To. Put. Me. Back. Together. I'm not a project you need to fix."

"I never thought you were, but you owe me some answers. Why didn't you say anything? You get so distracted that you didn't even think about me waiting for you? Or did you know I'd be there for you without giving a fuck about whatever consequences would come my way?"

He clenched his jaw, shaking his head.

"No," she said softly. "I don't need an answer, but you do. I was all in, Liam. You obviously weren't, and I'm only sorry I actually thought this was something that could work."

"You were all in?" His voice was heavy with disbelief. "I'm almost impressed you managed to say that with a straight face. You can tell yourself you were all in if you want, Leah, but you and I both know that's not the truth."

Her mouth dropped open. *He* was the one pushing her to focus on her art.

He held up a hand, stopping her response. "No, my turn. Let's pretend for a moment that you were all in, and I did tell you that my dad was in the hospital, and I couldn't make it out to take you to your show. You would've, what? Dropped everything to come to my side regardless of what I said I needed?"

She crossed her arms, taking a step back without thinking. "Probably. What's your point?"

He shrugged, a bitter smile sliding across his face. "Let's ignore the boundary issues right there."

He grinned sharply when he saw his words hit home. "You would've sabotaged your first step into the world you've been wanting for decades. And, eventually, you would've blamed me. You and I are both well aware chances like this don't come around that often. Excuse the fuck out of me if I'm not willing to give you the excuse to create the scenario that ends with you resenting me."

She shook her head. "So we're back to you making decisions for the both of us? I'm an adult. I can choose to put being there for you ahead of being at a show. It's not like there'd never be another chance."

"No," he said simply. "I'm making decisions for me. You aren't all in here, and this foolish attempt at a broken relationship is going to shatter whatever goodwill we managed to build. I'm not willing to take the risk when you have a safety net waiting for you."

"What safety net?" she asked, exasperated. "I'm right here."

"You still have your job at the firm. You still have one foot on your backup plan, and you can't pretend that's not the case. How many phone calls and emails have you fielded during your supposed sabbatical?

"You can't, or won't, decide what you want. You have the drive to make dreams come alive, but you're constantly chasing someone else's. You can't even commit to the art you've been pursuing for over a decade without wanting to drop it at the first sign of trouble."

She staggered back, his words landing like a physical blow.

He looked down at the counter separating them before shaking his head. "I'm not willing to be your excuse for why your dream didn't work out, and that's what you're setting me up to be, whether you realize it or not."

She looked away and wiped the tears from her cheeks, drawing in a shaky breath. "So that's it then."

"Yeah," he said softly, "that's it."

Leah's phone rang as she watched Alyssa Carlisle drive away with the horses. She'd been a bubbly person and had offered multiple assurances about the horses' new home.

Pulling the phone out of her back pocket, she frowned down at the contact photo she used for her firm, a dumpster on fire. Wondering how they were going to make her week worse, she briefly considered not answering.

After releasing a sigh, she forced a bright expression onto her face before answering. It was usually enough to fake a chipper tone. "Leah Carter, how can I help you?"

The voice on the other end came out breathy, almost panicked. "Leah, it's Madison."

Leah's fake smile dropped as worry overtook her. "What's wrong?"

"It's Mr. Cavalier, Mr. O'Neal's newest client. I think you met with him before... Anyway, his daughter's mom is planning to leave the state with their kid. No one here is able to help him with the emergency paperwork. O'Neal is out of town and asked if you could pinch hit for him. He's sorry to drop it in your lap, and I really hate to ask this with everything you have going on, but can you come in?"

Leah closed her eyes, massaging her temples as the familiar headache returned. "Yeah, I'll be in shortly."

"Thank you, Leah. I'm so sorry."

She shook her head. "Don't worry about it, Mads. Can you start the paperwork? I'm not going to be able to get there until early afternoon."

"On it. I have most of the information. I'll ask him to come in about two?"

"That should work. See if you can find someone to serve it. Everything else is filed?"

Madison sighed, frustration clear in her voice when she spoke again.

"Not quite yet. We were holding off, trying to come up with a settlement between the attorneys and clients. Mediation is scheduled for next week. I don't know what happened. Something made her bolt. She called the mediator to cancel the mediation, and the mediator called here to confirm.

"I checked in with her attorney, and she told me that Mrs. Cavalier just fired her. My contact there tells me she overheard some of it. It's the typical, nothing is going fast enough. You're going to lose me my kid, etc. She apparently decided to take matters into her own hands. Mr. Cavalier's got a friend who wasn't booted off Mrs. Cavalier's social media. That's how he found out about her plans to leave."

Leah blinked, mouth dropping open as she processed the slew of information. "Well, here's to hoping she doesn't pull that 'mother's rights' bullshit that one lady tried."

"With Judge H?"

Leah shuddered. "Yeah. I'm still not sure where that lady heard we were a 'mother county,' whatever that's supposed to mean. I can still hear the judge's lecture. It wasn't even directed at me, and still, fucking yikes. A person shouldn't be able to be that intimidating without raising their voice."

Madison laughed. "Yeah, I don't have any intention of having kids, and I'm still keeping that in mind. Never tell a judge they're supposed to be in your favor because you're the mother. I still wish I could've been there."

"Me too, girly. I would've traded places."

"No, you wouldn't."

Leah grinned. "Alright, no I wouldn't have. I'm headed out now. If you need me, give me a call. Not like I'll be able to do much in the car anyway."

"Will do. I'm really sorry, Leah."

"Hey, don't worry about it. I knew I might have to come back for something like this when I asked to take a sabbatical to play around with the farm."

"Still, this sucks, and I'm sorry to have to pull you into it. Drive safe."

By early evening, Madison and Leah had Mr. Cavalier out the door with the emergency order in hand, ready to deliver to the Sheriff's Department. Leah leaned back in her office chair, studying the ceiling as she waited for her brain to come back online. Exhaustion weighed her down. She closed her eyes and massaged her temples, hoping the headache wouldn't develop into the migraine she was dreading.

"I don't know if I can keep doing this, Mads."

"Preach, lady. Family law is a madhouse. Still wishing you had gone the paralegal route instead?"

Leah laughed softly. "Nope. I don't think it would've been much better."

"Less anxiety. Not being the one making the decisions or recommendations is nice."

Leah smiled, looking over at Madison. "Are you trying to tell me this day wasn't stressful for you?'

Madison laughed brightly. "Hell no, lady. I need to decompress. Come back to my place?"

Madison cleared her throat before pausing the show.

Leah jolted at the abrupt sound, almost dropping the chip she had just finagled the perfect amount of dip onto. They'd been watching *Leverage*, decompressing from the day's tribulations with mocktails and snacks.

"Well, that's ominous."

Madison gave her a reassuring grin that did absolutely nothing to reassure. "I was just thinking we hadn't covered a maybe important topic."

Leah narrowed her eyes. Where was this going?

"So," Madison said slowly, "how's the boy?"

Leah popped the chip into her mouth. Gesturing that she was chewing and therefore clearly couldn't answer, she shrugged and widened her eyes.

Madison scowled and rolled her eyes. "I will wait, you walnut."

When she finished chewing, Leah stuck her tongue out at Madison.

Madison blew her a raspberry and poked her in the side.

Dodging the next poke, Leah gave in. "Fine, fine," she said, rushing the words out. "He missed the show because his dad was in the hospital. And he broke up with me because he wasn't going to be my excuse if I walked away from my dreams, I'm constantly chasing someone else's dream, and I wasn't really all in."

Madison whistled, raising both eyebrows. "Shit."

Leah sighed deeply. "Yeah. And you know the worst part?"

Madison shook her head slowly. "Tell me."

"He was right. Not about everything. But having a safety net and maybe not being all in? I'm so scared I'm not good enough that, yeah, maybe I *was* looking for a point of failure that wasn't me. And with the farm?"

She groaned, covering her face with her hands. "What if I hate it? It was supposed to be me and Sadie, not just me." She dropped her hands. "So, yeah. He's right. I am still holding on to the firm. Just in case. I basically had one foot out the door, and he doesn't have an exit plan, especially with his position at the college."

"That he jeopardized all by himself."

Leah grimaced. "True. But he did a lot to help me out at Sadie's. I would've gone insane trying to juggle everything by myself. I'm going to hold up my end. Help him as much as I can with the tenure bid."

Madison nodded slowly, watching Leah carefully. "Did you tell him that?"

"Tell him what?"

"That you're still willing to hold up your side of the bargain after he broke up with you?"

Leah frowned. "No. I was not in a great place when we saw each other last and hadn't even thought about it. I should talk to him." She grabbed her tablet from the side table.

"Are you going to send him an official email, Miss Carter?" Madison asked, laughter in her voice.

Leah snorted. "No, I'm going to send my notice to the partners."

Madison's mouth dropped open. "You're quitting?"

Leah bit her lip and nodded. "No more safety net."

Madison watched in silence as Leah typed out her resignation before wiggling the tablet. "Proofread, please?"

"Absolutely." She grinned, making grabby hands at the tablet.

Leah handed it over with a laugh. This felt right. She watched as Madison read through it, correcting a word here and there before handing it back.

"Good to go, girl."

Leah smiled. "Thanks, Mads."

"You're welcome. Are you actually going to send it?"

Leah chewed on her lip, staring at the tablet. "Yeah," she said finally, pressing the send icon gently. It was done. No going back. Panic and freedom whirled inside her as she stared blankly at the screen.

Madison squealed and pulled her into a hug that quickly turned into a crazy dance around her living room.

"Oh my God," Leah said breathlessly. "I can't believe I did that."

Madison's smile spread across her face. "Me neither. Way to go!"

Leah rested her hand against her rapidly beating heart. The ping of an incoming email made her jump with a soft curse. She smiled softly when she pulled up the message. One of the senior partners wishing her well. She skimmed over the date information, wondering why the partner was sending an email so late. "Oh, shit."

"What, what's wrong?"

Leah looked back at her, eyes wide. "It's Wednesday."

"Yes," Madison agreed slowly.

"Liam's work reception is tonight."

"Shit," Madison agreed. "Shit, shit, shit. What time does it start? Do you have enough time to get there?"

"If I leave now, I'll be acceptably late, but I can't go like this." She gestured down at her jeans and casual shirt, eyes wide.

Madison looked around her apartment, drumming her hand against her thigh as she thought. "Wait," she said, snapping her fingers. "Your dress from the firm's client appreciation cocktail party. I still have it."

She dashed out of the room and returned with Leah's red formfitting, off-the-shoulder cocktail dress.

"Do you think it's a bit much?" Leah asked, eyes flicking between the dress and Madison.

"I think it's better than what you're wearing. Go; get changed, and leave. I'll pack your office for you."

"Thank you," Leah blurted. "You have my apartment key?"

"Yes, Leah. Go," Madison said urgently.

Leah grabbed the dress and her purse before dashing to the bathroom. After changing quickly, she bundled her clothes under her arm and raced out the door, calling out one last thank you to Madison before she left.

Chapter Twenty: The Ball

A wolf whistle pierced the quiet night air. She jumped, fumbling the phone in her hand. She'd seen enough to note her message to Liam remained unread. Looking sharply in the direction of the whistle, her sharp retort about respecting a person's autonomy died on her tongue.

"Stunning," Ros said with a warm grin. "Liam won't know what hit him."

Leah flushed at the compliment. "Thanks, Ros. Have you seen him?"

She nodded to the venue's double doors. "He's talking to Sheldon and Dennis. You should hustle in. He cleans up almost as well as you do."

After giving Ros a quick hug, she did as instructed. Liam, Sheldon, and Dennis were talking by the bar. Smoothing her dress, she strode over to them. Sliding her hand down Liam's arm when she reached him, she nodded to the other two men. Out of the corner of her eye, she caught Liam's brief look of surprise before Sheldon spoke.

"Leah," he said warmly, "we were just asking Liam where you were."

She smiled back at him. "What excuse did he give you?"

"We hadn't gotten that far yet. Poor boy was starting to look uncomfortable before you showed up." Looking her up and down, Dennis winked. "Whatever the reason, I'm sure I'm not the only one who thinks you're well worth the wait."

She smiled. "It's my charming personality you're referencing, right?"

"Oh, absolutely, darling," Dennis agreed.

Sheldon bumped his shoulder against his husband's, rolling his eyes. "I would've expected Liam to wait for you, especially if it were a simple matter of taking a little longer to get ready than anticipated."

Leah's blush returned at the gentle inquiry, and she instinctively shifted toward Liam. He pulled her closer with an arm around her waist, and she leaned into him. "I was called into the office for an emergency project. The lead attorney on the case is out of the country, and they needed a quick turnaround. I decompressed with a friend after everything wrapped up, and I completely lost track of time."

Dennis raised an eyebrow. "Is this friend trying to drag you back into the fold early?"

A startled bark of laughter escaped her at the question. "No, actually. She's of the camp that I should run fast and far."

"Oooo, I like this girl already," Dennis said with a grin.

Sheldon bumped his husband's shoulder. "Shouldn't we be asking if she enjoys the job first?"

Dennis snorted. "She's a family law lawyer."

"Hey now, some of us enjoy the profession."

"Are you seriously trying to claim to be one of those who enjoy the profession?" Dennis asked, arching a skeptical eyebrow.

Leah shrugged and wrinkled her nose. "Some of us enjoy the profession."

Liam squeezed her softly in a sideways hug. "Well, I think that's about all we're going to get out of the counselor. Should we discuss politics next?"

The rest of the night passed in a whirlwind of small talk, comments about the dress, and discussing the upcoming shrimp boil and play combo. When they could make a graceful exit, Liam walked her back to her car.

"Thanks for coming," he said softly, brushing a strand of hair back behind her ear.

She looked into the windows of the hall before nodding. "I'm sorry I didn't tell you I would. I was a little caught up in everything."

He glanced up at the night sky before settling his gaze back on hers. "You didn't have to come." He held up a hand when she started to speak. "And don't say a deal is a deal. The way I left it, you didn't have to come."

"Yeah, I know. I wanted to."

He sighed, studying her carefully. "Thank you, Lee."

She smiled wryly, glancing back at the hall out of the corner of her eye. "You're welcome."

"Sheldon's sending me out of town tomorrow."

"That's fantastic, Liam. Looking good on the tenure again, then?"

He shrugged and waffled his hand. "Maybe? He wants me to handle the summer class excursion. Apparently, the original professor decided to bolt because he was offered a tenure position at another college. The festival they planned to cover as part of the class goals is tomorrow."

"Ooo," she said, voice teasing, "a festival. You love those."

He groaned, letting his head fall forward. "Don't remind me." When he straightened, she restrained herself from pushing the hair out of his eyes. "I owe you an apology."

She wrinkled her nose. "You know, I don't recall apologizing myself, so I think we can call it even."

He cocked an eyebrow. "Those dogs did cause damage, and the goats ate several important notes."

She raised both eyebrows back at him, eyes dancing with her suppressed laughter. "Hey, you brought them into this. They almost burned my house down first. And I had *nothing* to do with the goats. I don't even know where they came from."

His lips quirked up before he smoothed his expression. "You had my car towed."

She rolled her lips into her mouth and bit down to prevent the smile from erupting. When she could compose herself, she poked him in the chest. "You made me get a citation. I had a perfect record before that."

At his deadpan look, she burst out laughing. "I had a perfect record *as an adult*, you asshole."

He gave her a boyish grin in return before he sighed, expression darkening. "I'll miss your Hail Mary tomorrow. If you want me to skip it, say the word. Sheldon will understand."

She arched an eyebrow. Sheldon was great, but he wouldn't understand. And Dennis wasn't the type to interfere with his spouse's business, so they didn't have an out. But she couldn't say that. Clearly, he was already feeling indebted to her for simply showing up.

"I've got it covered, but thank you."

He studied her carefully. "You sure?"

She smiled brightly. "Of course I'm sure."

Walking up the porch steps that night, she gasped. A gorgeous slab of live edge cherry wood was leaning against the wall next to her front door. Moving closer, she skated her fingers from the rough bark to the smooth dark wood. It was *stunning*. Her mind whirled with the scenes she could burn into it.

A small card was propped up on its edge, leaning against the wall. She opened it carefully, pulling out the card with a soft shush of paper against paper.

I'm sorry. Bright side? I thought I'd be apologizing with walnut by now.

She bit her lip. So did she. While they dated, his big apologies came in the form of wood for her art. Her apologies had been special editions of his favorite books.

Out of habit, she flipped the card to the back. She shouldn't have expected anything more, but there it was.

Confession: I wish it was walnut.

Chapter Twenty-One: Final Call

"You're ready. You've done everything you can to prepare for today."

Leah paced across the cabin, pressing her hand against her churning stomach as she spoke with Cassidy. "I'm worried."

"It's going to work, or it won't."

"Yeah, the 'or it won't' is what has me worried." She shook her head, looking up at the ceiling as she tried to stave off the looming tears. "Shit. This is as bad as waiting for a trial to start."

"Lee," Cassidy's voice came back, calm and firm. "If the possibility of losing the farm, which is what you think is at stake—*even though it isn't* because we would definitely figure something else out—is the same as waiting for a hearing, then you really never should have been a lawyer."

Leah stopped pacing to laugh, collapsing down into the couch. "Well, yes, or at least not practice family law, but we already knew that."

"Yes," Cassidy said primly, "we did. We also know this day is going to be whatever it is. If you don't find the right partner or investor here, we still have time to think of something else. I'm just sorry we couldn't be there with you, help with the madness."

"You're doing exactly what I need you to be doing. Besides, I'm going to have so many people here helping out with everything that we're going to be tripping over each other. These theater kids…"

She cut herself off, wrinkling her nose before she continued in a contemplative tone. "I feel old now. Half of them are in college or about to be. Anyway, they're awesome. Three of them have done shrimp boils with their families, so they're going to handle the actual cooking. Several have an impeccable eye for design, which is great."

"Of course," Cassidy agreed, laughter in her voice.

"They were out yesterday to set up the tables and everything. Looks awesome, by the way. I took a bunch of pictures. Sam has the stage built. All of the tickets are prepaid. It's just going to be a matter of cooking, serving, and schmoozing."

"Exactly," Cassidy said.

Leah blushed, covering her eyes with her hand. "You manipulative little shit. Ugh," she added, "I hate schmoozing."

Cassidy's laughter rang out, lifting Leah's spirits. "You know it. And you will be *talking*, which you are very good at, not *schmoozing*. You're selling something these people already want. A phenomenal business opportunity on gorgeous land."

"Right," Leah said faintly.

"You got this. Now say it."

"I've got this," Leah murmured.

"Maybe try it one more time and actually mean it, dear."

Leah snorted. "I've got this."

"There's my girl."

"We've totally got this," Leah told herself, voice faint. Straightening her spine, she took the power pose recommended in the last Continuing Legal Education course she took. She repeated herself, almost managing to maintain a straight face and serious tone before she collapsed in a fit of giggles. At least the laughter was only a little hysterical.

Fortunately for her peace of mind, she sobered enough to tamp down the deranged look and grab the bags full of food before Dennis pulled up.

Six theater kids piled out of the van, waving and grinning at Leah. Mallory, a member of the theater group heavily blessed with both common sense and leadership skills, bounced on her toes, grinning broadly.

Dennis hopped out, joining the kids at the side of the van before clapping his hands together. "Alright. We ready for this?"

"Aye, aye, Captain," they chorused.

"Oh, here," Mallory said, stepping up to Leah, "let me grab some of those bags." Connor, Travis, and Trevor followed suit, leaving Leah without any bags.

She blinked, finding herself with suddenly empty arms. "I can carry some of them."

"Well, yes," Dennis agreed. "But why?"

Leah laughed. "Fair point." Gesturing toward the barn, she asked, "Shall we start walking over, so they can be relieved of their burdens?"

On the way to the barn, she realized they had left a question unanswered. "Who did we decide was in charge of the cooking?"

Mallory raised her hand from ahead and to the right of Leah. "I was elected for some reason."

Trevor laughed softly, walking by her side. "Ah, yes, for some reason unknown to all." When she gave him a sideways look and raised an eyebrow, he rolled his eyes.

"What?" she asked. "I've literally never made this before, and the three of you have."

"True," Connor agreed from her left. "But you're the most organized and really good at the whole giving direction, herding cats thing."

Mallory frowned over at him. "I'm not bossy."

"No, ma'am," Travis piped up from behind. "Boss material, though, definitely." When everyone else chorused their agreement, Leah was close enough to see Mallory blush, clearly pleased.

Dennis drifted in Leah's direction. She slowed to match his pace, allowing the theater crew to pull ahead toward the buffet table they had set up outside the barn. Ros had warned her that the smell of the shrimp boil would permeate the space, so they'd cook it outside. Mallory immediately took charge, efficiently dispatching the crew. They'd have it handled in record time.

Dennis grinned, watching them. "They're adorable, right?"

"Uh, yeah," she said softly. "So freaking cute. Any of them dating?"

"Finally," he exclaimed, "someone other than the teachers to dish with. So, Travis and Brian graduated last year. They're heading to college out of state. Trevor and Mallory are going into their senior year. If they're dating in any combination, they've managed to keep it quiet."

Watching as the four moved around each other easily, he added, "I totally ship it."

Leah laughed, stopping for a moment to look over at him. "Are teachers supposed to ship their students?"

He shrugged. "We do it all the damn time, babe. You and Liam were apparently the topic of a lot of debate when we were in school."

Her mouth dropped open, and she looked over at him with wide eyes. "Tell me you're joking."

He shook his head slowly. "Nope," he answered, popping the "p."

She grabbed his arm lightly, keeping him in place. "What are they saying now?"

He scratched his head, studying her. "Are you sure you want to know?"

"No," she answered. "But tell me anyway."

He laughed. "Okay, so there's three camps. First camp, it would've worked the first time, if it was going to work at all. Second camp, oh good, they've gotten a second chance at such a sweet romance. First camp is divided on whether or not they actually like the two of you as a couple."

She narrowed her eyes, studying him. "And the third camp?"

He put a hand over his heart theatrically. "I don't know if I can violate the sanctity of teacher prep conferences to tell you."

She raised her eyebrows, studying him. "What if I tell you something that might sway the first camp?"

"Oooo, well, I could possibly be persuaded. Tell me, and I'll decide if it's worth it."

"Nope." She crossed her arms. "It's worth it."

He shook his head. "I don't know."

She shrugged and started walking toward the barn again. "Okay, I won't tell you."

"Whoa, whoa, wait. Alright, I'll tell you," he agreed, stopping her.

She spun around to face him. "Spill it, Mister."

"Okay, fine, but you're not going to like it."

She put a hand on her hip and raised a single eyebrow.

"The third camp thinks you're faking it."

Her mouth dropped open. "Oh my God, seriously?"

"Yeah. We've all read a few too many romances, I think. The timing just seemed too convenient, the forgiveness a little too fast."

"Are you in that third camp?" she asked suspiciously.

His mouth opened and closed a few times before he answered, "Well, yes. I, too, have read many a romance. I think it's absolutely adorable, if you're faking it or not."

She sighed and looked away, pulling a hand back through her hair and shaking her head.

"Your turn to dish. What's going to sway that first camp?"

She glanced back at him out of the corner of her eye. "My mom was convinced he was going to ruin my life if we stayed together, so she interfered."

"You're kidding."

"Nope," she answered, also popping the "p." "Just found out."

"Well, damn," he said softly.

"Yeah," she agreed. "Let's go get our marching orders."

Leah gave Ros a tired grin and leaned into her side hug. The hours had flown by in a blur of people arriving, potential investors, play-goers, and what seemed to be the majority of the town. They'd settled on two runs of the dinner and show.

Leah had been most delighted by watching the play and speaking with the townspeople. They'd exclaimed over the setup, telling her this should be an annual event. She hadn't figured out how it would work to clear out the arena for the time frame needed for the play when the most interest from the potential investors was in full-time boarding and lessons. She'd keep working on it.

Ros had been a huge help with making the rounds for each of the potential investors. She knew which were most interested in the trails or the boarding. She'd restrained herself to one sly comment about finding a couple patrons of the arts instead, should Leah ultimately decide to gracefully concede that she was meant to focus on her art, not running Sadie's farm. Leah had rolled her eyes at the time, but she had to admit, even if only to herself, that it would be nice to be an old-timey artist with a couple patrons to keep her in art supplies.

"How are you doing?"

"Good. Tired. I wish..." she trailed off, not entirely sure what she'd wish for anyway.

"You wish that we could've gotten a high enough offer that you could hire someone to be a barn manager, freeing you up to focus on your dream come true instead of Sadie's?"

Leah winced. Ros had, as usual, hit the nail on the head. "I feel awful thinking it."

She'd met with the first round of potential investors during the second dinner. It was promising. The only downside was the time that would be needed on her end. She did not have the financing available to hire a manager, so the responsibilities would fall to her.

From her time with Sadie, she had a good idea of the time commitment it would take. Her time at the firm had taught her how much a mentally draining job took away from her ability to focus on the art.

"You shouldn't. Sadie wouldn't have wanted you killing yourself to follow her dream. She wanted to see you chasing yours. She just thought she'd have more time to push you that way."

She sighed, eyes focused on the cars pulling out. She had the contact information for all of the potential investors. She'd need to contact them within the next few days, hammer out the details on who could offer what. The money available from the potential investors would outfit the barn and cover the necessary repairs to host multiple horses year-round. The monthly income from boarding and hosting lessons would be sufficient to refinance the mortgage with a different bank. It was tight but doable.

"I'll make it work." She waved her hand around. "I can't give up this farm. It means the world to me. I can't explain how much peace I feel just pulling up the driveway. It's worth a few uncomfortable years. "Who knows? It could cash flow enough to hire a barn manager in less than three years."

"What about that idea Bryon, Clara, and her troupe of yogis had? To turn this place into an event venue and weekend camp with rentals to other people as the opportunities arise? It would take less time from you, especially with Clara already volunteering to coordinate."

Leah let out a soft laugh, wishing she felt the humor to match the sound. "If we had the money to make it happen, it would be a dream come true."

She cast Ros a tired grin. "Let's go back inside and watch round two."

Ros laughed. "Alright, girlie. I'll let you off the hook."

Leah widened her eyes and placed a hand over her heart in faux innocence. "Maybe I just really loved the play and want to watch it again immediately."

Ros nodded skeptically. "Uh-huh. And you're not going to the one tomorrow?"

Leah laughed, genuinely amused. She linked her arm through Ros's. "I *am* going to tomorrow's run. But I am going to seize the available escape from thinking."

The two women came to an abrupt stop when they spotted the trio exiting the barn. Clara and Byron were escorting someone with a familiar face.

"Leah," Clara said warmly, "you remember Will Alderson, right? He said he met with you at your gallery exhibition at Tasha's place."

"I do. It's a pleasure seeing you here, Will." She gestured to Rosalee. "This is my dear friend, Rosalee."

She watched Byron and Clara as Ros and Will exchanged pleasantries. Byron was rocking forward onto his toes and back onto his heels. Clara was watching her husband with fond amusement but was clearly excited. Leah's eyes crinkled with her smile at the couple. These two were couple goals, no question.

She tore her attention back to Will as his conversation with Ros lulled.

"Did you find the place alright?"

He grinned. "I did, thank you. It's really lovely country you've got out here. I only wish I had gotten here early enough to join the hike. I thought it would only be horse riders out there today."

Leah laughed lightly. "So did I. I wish I could have given you a heads-up. It was a very impromptu hike. A few yogis heard about this place from Clara."

She nodded in the other woman's direction. Clara beamed, straightening under the attention. "Clara, Byron, and Rosalee have all been a huge help in getting this in order. They've been spit-balling ideas for this place since I mentioned I was looking for investors."

Clara smiled warmly. "I have several yoga instructor friends who were close to town and interested in seeing the play anyway. We were planning to practice yoga on the lawn, if there were too many horseback riders for a hike to make sense."

"Always good to have a backup plan," Will said with a smile.

Leah ducked her head in agreement. "Most of the time. What did you think of the play?"

"It was wonderful. I'm almost as impressed by the potential for this place as I was with your art."

She flushed at the unexpected praise. "Thank you; that's so kind of you to say."

He gave her a lopsided smile. "Simply the truth. Clara, Byron, and I have been talking a bit. I have to say, I really love the direction their thoughts are headed. I've heard a lot of people talking about the potential for long-term boarding and horse-riding lessons, which would, of course, be a great avenue for you to pursue.

"However, I couldn't help but notice how much you seemed to enjoy yourself tonight. And how much time running a barn would take away from your art. You have a gift, Leah. I would very much like to work with you on commissioning a series of pieces. To that end, it seems like there might be a path forward that leaves you with some time to spare."

Leah's mind whirred at the mention of commissioning her for some pieces. He'd mentioned his interest at the gallery, but she hadn't heard anything since that night. She thought he had met with Tasha and changed his mind. People talked about being interested in commissioning art but usually balked at the price.

He smiled softly. "Sorry if that was a surprise. I had a series of meetings to attend to, but I assure you I'm very interested in working out a deal with you to commission some large pieces along with smaller pieces to integrate. I prefer to go through Tasha as an initial contact. I've found it works better for the artist and myself if we have an intermediary for the initial steps."

She was blown away. Her wildest dream was to have sold something at the show and to garner enough interest to sell future pieces. A commission of several pieces from someone who clearly had experience in purchasing art wasn't something she'd dared to dream.

"That sounds amazing. Thank you. Really, thank you. That's a huge compliment to me."

His eyes crinkled charmingly when he smiled. "I think we can both look forward to a beneficial arrangement for the art. Whether we collaborate here is, of course, an entirely separate question. Based on what I've heard, you have options. Whether you choose to explore a potential partnership on this project has no bearing on my interest in commissioning you.

"I have some money to spare to invest into projects I think are worthwhile, and this definitely seems worthwhile. I may be biased by my desire to ensure you'll have time to fulfill my dreams of seeing your pieces in my buildings. That said, Clara and Byron paint an excellent picture of this place's potential."

"Wow. That... That sounds absolutely amazing. I've adored all of the ideas they've come up with so far. Do you want to get together soon to go over details, see if we'd work well together?"

"I actually have to head out of town tomorrow morning." He ducked his head. "I really need to win my former assistant back. She was the brains behind schedule management for sure. If you could spare some time to meet tonight, I'd love to hash out some ideas, give each of us a direction to look for the cost estimates, and we can keep up the discussion via email and perhaps video-conferencing. Does that work for you?"

"Absolutely," Leah agreed.

Clara and Byron beamed.

Mallory bounced on her toes, watching the last of the taillights disappear down the driveway. "That was awesome," she gushed. "We should clean up and then head to the after party."

Turning to Leah, her eyes dancing and cheeks flushed, she asked, "You'll join us, right?"

"Whoa, no," Leah said. When Mallory looked a little hurt, she rushed to clarify. "Everything here can wait until tomorrow morning. Go to the party. Celebrate. I'm beat, and I need sleep." She winked, adding, "Getting older has some benefits, but lasting energy is not one of them."

"Are you sure?" Mallory asked, brows furrowing.

"I'm positive, Mallory," Leah assured with a smile. At least someone should have a night filled with celebration of a job well done rather than churning anxiety over whether it would be *enough*.

"And you're sure you don't want to join us? It could help keep your mind off things."

Leah laughed. "You are wise beyond your years. I'm sure, but thank you. I had a lot of fun tonight, and I don't know what I would have done without all of you." She nodded toward the rest of the crew. "Don't let them leave you in the dust."

Mallory grinned before darting off, slinging her arms around Travis and Trevor when she caught up to them.

When their taillights disappeared around the bend, she took a deep breath, assuring herself it would be fine. She didn't have to make any decisions tonight. She spun around and shut the doors to the barn. Everything in there would be fine until tomorrow.

Bouncing her thumb against her thigh as she walked, she tried very hard to not think. Will Alderson's offer was a dream come true. Maybe too good to be true. He hadn't mentioned any numbers, but he also hadn't balked at the list of projects Byron had rattled off like a grocery list. His lack of concern *could* stem from inexperience in this particular realm of business.

And who was she anyway to think she should follow this idea just because it seemed more exciting? The boarding idea had much more reliable income. At least three of the loan officers she spoke with would offer her financing based on the proven business model. But an event venue with temporary camping and horse-riding trips? The revenue there wasn't nearly as easy to estimate.

But it would be fun. Seeing new people roll in every week. Slow it down in the winter. Have the time to really focus on her art. See what she could do with the time and materials. And Will's reiterated desire for the commissioned pieces. Depending on the commission size, she could theoretically drain her retirement accounts and refinance based upon anticipated revenue from her art.

It wasn't enough, though. An artist's income was too inconsistent. She dropped her head back with a groan as she walked. What was she thinking quitting when she did? She could've drained her retirement accounts, used the income from her reliable job to refinance the mortgage and *then* quit. It would've bought her more time. Of course, she also might've stayed, then.

Probably would have stayed. It would've been skeevy to have that as a plan.

She shut the cabin door behind herself, leaning back against it with her hands covering her eyes. This not thinking plan really worked out great. Alright. New strategy. She'd run the numbers on the plan she'd crafted with Byron, Clara, and Will. She'd wait to send them until the morning so as not to look like a total psycho.

Tomorrow, she'd send off a different set of numbers and projections to the investors most interested in helping her launch a boarding and lessons business. Once she heard back from all of them, she'd schedule appointments with some loan officers. Figure out what they'd need from her. Or maybe Will would reply, swoop in with all the cash, and she'd be set to dance through the fields and follow her dreams. She laughed at herself, shaking her head.

And pigs would fly.

Leah climbed out of bed with an irritated scowl on her face, cursing her anxiety and its predictable interference with her sleep. Knowing she wouldn't be falling asleep until she was truly exhausted, she threw on sweatpants and a large sweatshirt over her pajama shirt. She'd tackle the barn.

The wax paper had already been disposed of during intermission, and everyone had been good about throwing away candy wrappers and tossing cans into the trash cans set aside for recycling. Leah frowned, hands on her hips as she surveyed the space. There wasn't much to do. With a sigh, she knotted the large bags of trash and recycling to haul to the appropriate dumpsters hidden behind hedges in the front yard.

Returning to the barn, she turned on her playlist, intentionally ignoring any notifications, and returned her phone to her back pocket. She pulled the tablecloths off and piled them in the office next to the stacked dishes. After the tables were clear and folded, she moved them into an empty stall. The pleasant music and physical labor of hauling away the no longer necessary tables served to steer her mood in the right direction. Standing back to look at the small number of empty stalls remaining, she bumped up dealing with the items in the stalls on the mental priorities list.

After clearing the arena, she grabbed the tablecloths. Of course, she dropped one on the way to the cabin and needed to chase it down. One measly scrap of wind in the otherwise still night, and it had to be right there. Snatching it with a huff, she returned to the pile she'd dropped on the ground. Holding them securely, she grumbled to herself until she reached the basement. She froze, staring at the rumpled bedding.

Shifting the tablecloths into a two-handed hold against her stomach, she stared at the bed before looking up at the ceiling, blinking the tears out of her eyes. "When am I going to catch a break? Like, really. I could use one at any time here, universe. Please and fuck you very much."

After a silent moment, she muttered an apology for the cursing.

Huffing at herself, she shoved the tablecloths into the empty basket sitting next to the washer before stripping the sheets and comforter off the bed. Pushing them aggressively into the washer, she frowned down at the bundled mess before adding detergent and softener, slamming the lid closed, and starting the machine.

She propped her forearm against one of the rungs of the ladder before resting her forehead against her bent arm. She breathed in for a count of five, held her breath for a count of seven, and exhaled for a count of eight until she felt less like she was going to dissolve into a puddle of tears any second. She'd been close to settled. She just needed to do more, exhaust herself until she was ready to drop.

After hauling all of the dishes in from the barn, she turned up her music on her phone to tackle the piles one by one. She sank into the chore, bobbing her head to the music and losing track of time. A knock at the front door made her jump with a shriek, dropping the bowl she'd been working on back into the sink with a soapy splash. Drying her hands, she took a deep breath, waiting a moment for her heart to stop rabbiting in her chest.

Glancing at the clock, she frowned in confusion. Who would be here at three in the morning? Her heartbeat resumed its gallop at the idea someone she loved was hurt again, and she rushed to pull the door open.

At the sight of Liam, she blinked several times before blurting, "What's wrong?"

He took a step back before holding up calming hands. "Nothing you don't already know about."

She pressed her hand against her chest, feeling her heart pound frantically against her sternum. "Okay," she said slowly, "then what are you doing here?"

"I wanted to talk to you," he said carefully.

She stepped back slightly, shaking her head. "And it couldn't wait until morning?" She waved a hand before adding, "Normal people morning."

"It could, and I was going to, but I got some texts," he said slowly, as if he were thinking through how much to share with her.

She crossed her arms over her chest, frowning. "From which cousin?"

He winced, cocking his head to the side as he clearly debated the relative merits of throwing whichever cousin it was under the bus or refusing to tell her.

She raised an expectant eyebrow, tapping her foot as she waited.

"All of them," he answered, tone rising at the end as if asking a question.

"Seriously," she blinked rapidly as she processed the information, "all of them?"

"Well, not all of them. All of the important ones."

She blinked several times, processing the information. "Even Derek?"

"Yeah," he answered, tone wry.

"Jesus," she muttered, turning to head back into the kitchen. "Come on in, then, I guess."

She held up a finger without turning back around. "Make one smart-ass comment, and you're going right back out that door."

"Fair enough," he muttered, following her into the cabin.

He surveyed the remaining dishes. "Want me to dry?"

She sighed. He wasn't going to just turn around and leave, regardless of what she claimed to want. "Yes, please."

"What happened to the trip? Or," she added, waving a soapy hand, "what brings you back so late? Or early, I guess."

"Uh, nothing. It was fine."

She raised an eyebrow. "College couldn't spring for a hotel?"

"They did. I just..." He trailed off, focused on scrubbing the plate in his hands before he shrugged. "I wanted to come back. See if you were awake."

"At three in the morning?" she asked, voice heavy with disbelief.

His eyes darted to hers before returning to the next dish in his hands. "If you weren't awake, your disbelief would be more compelling."

Her lips twisted into a wry smile. "Fair enough. So, here we are."

He nodded slowly, eyes focused on his task. "I don't want to break up. I'm in love with you. I've never stopped being in love with you."

She stilled, the dish in her hands slipping back beneath the suds. "That was never our problem."

She could practically feel his sigh from beside her. "I never should have accused you of not being all in."

"Well, you were right. I had a fallback plan, and I wasn't all in with our relationship or my art. I would've missed the deadline and a major opportunity if you hadn't pushed me to take the time to finish that piece."

She glanced at him out of the corner of her eye. He was studying her, dishes abandoned.

"I handed in my resignation last week. Madison cleaned out my office for me. I'll go back next week to help transition some of the files and pick up my final paycheck, and then I'm done."

He blinked rapidly, taking a step backwards. "You didn't have to do that."

"I know," she said simply. "I did it for me."

"And now you don't have a fallback plan," he said softly.

She scoffed. "Yeah, that about sums it up."

"I'm sorry, Lee."

Tears sprang to her eyes as she shook her head. "Well, it's hardly your fault," she said, voice cracking.

"Still." He drew her into his arms. She tucked her head under his chin, allowing the tears to come as she buried her face into his chest.

She woke to light streaming through the window and Liam lightly stroking her back. They'd moved to the couch. He'd held her until she calmed down, and they talked. Sometime during the night, he had rearranged them so he was lying across the couch below her. She sighed, snuggling down into his chest. After feeling the rumble of his "good morning" from beneath her, she mumbled a reply.

"What are we going to do?"

She sighed, wanting to delay this conversation but knowing it needed to happen. "Do we get a third chance?" she asked.

She could feel him shift below her as he considered. "I think," he said slowly, "this still counts as our second chance. And if it doesn't, we get all the chances we want to take."

She propped herself up, folding her forearms across his chest to study him. "Huh. I like it. Philosophical, almost. That's kind of hot."

He grinned, eyes twinkling in the morning light. "You think a lot of things are kind of hot."

She pursed her lips, studying him. "This is true. Some of them you even agree with."

His grin turned wicked. "A lot of them I agree with."

She hummed, eyes flicking from his lips to his eyes before she raised an eyebrow. "Are you thinking of something in particular?"

"I might be."

She laughed softly. "Care to share with the class, Professor?"

He sat up slowly, giving her enough time to wrap her legs around his waist as he settled into a seated position against the armrest. He cradled her face with his palm, drawing her into a soft kiss. Feathering kisses down her neck after they drew apart, he spoke between kisses. "Something about me on my knees, if I remember correctly."

She swallowed, leaning her forehead against his shoulder as molten heat shot to her core. She bit her bottom lip before responding, angling her head to grant him better access to her neck. "I don't know if I would call you on your knees kind of hot."

"No?" He paused his efforts to drive her mad only long enough to ask.

She swallowed roughly as he gently sucked right behind her ear. Shit, she was already wet. "No. I, uh... Fuck," she groaned. "Like that."

His hands skated down her sides, and she rocked against him. What was she saying? She pulled her scattered thoughts together. A finger dipping below her waistband stole her breath.

What were they talking about?

She felt his smile against her neck as he dipped his finger inside. "You're so wet for me, sweetheart."

She clenched against the digit, grinding down as she panted. Stars burst in front of her eyes before she finally remembered. Him on his knees.

"Right," she gasped, stilling her slow grind. "That's definitely hot, no qualifiers necessary."

"Ah, excellent," he purred. "Let's do that then."

She nodded, words abandoning her.

He shifted, lifting her in his arms before placing her gently on the sofa as he slid to his knees. Her breath caught. Sliding her hand into his hair, she pulled him forward into another kiss. He went easily, groaning as her fingers tightened.

She started pulling his shirt up, fingers skating along heated flesh as she did. When they parted, he tossed his shirt aside, eyes immediately finding her again. She drank in the sight of his broad shoulders and muscled chest, leaning forward to bite softly against his neck, running her hands across his shoulders and down his arms to tangle with his hands.

She released her hold on him when he reached her waistband. Their eyes locked as he slowly drew her pants and underwear down and off before pulling her hips to the edge of the couch. She brushed her foot against his side, arching an eyebrow. "Fair is fair."

He swallowed, drinking in the sight of her before stripping off his jeans and black briefs, pushing them to the side to join hers. Her mouth watered, and she licked her lips to wet them.

He bent forward, rolling his eyes up to look at her as he pressed a kiss to the arch of her foot before moving up her leg. She clenched the blanket beneath her as he traveled up one leg, kissing, sucking, and biting lightly. His tongue swirling behind her knee made her jerk with a soft cry.

He skipped her wet center to make his way back down the other leg just as slowly, driving her crazy. She cursed when he finally turned his attention to her soaked core, licking around her lips before flicking his tongue against her clitoris at the same time he pushed two long fingers inside her, crooking them at just the right spot to make her see stars.

"Fuck, fuck, fuck," she moaned as her orgasm crashed through her. A new moan stuttered out of her when it kept going, waves of sensation flowing through her as he coaxed her further. She floated back to Earth, blinking languidly until her vision cleared. She wet her lips, staring down at him, her ankles crossed behind his back, one heel digging into the center. He pulled back from her with a wicked smirk before wiping away the moisture.

Her core clenched again, hard, when he drew two fingers into his mouth before releasing them with a wet pop. The mischief dancing in his eyes told her he knew *exactly* what he was doing to her.

She swallowed roughly, sliding her feet back to the floor. Eyes on him, she pulled herself forward and down into his lap. Her hand around his cock confirmed he'd already pulled on a condom. Good, she didn't want to wait any longer.

Gaze locked with his, she guided him into her with the hand still wrapped around him. Slowly, oh so slowly, she sank down, gasping as he filled her.

Chapter Twenty-Two: Hail Mary, Take Two

Leah groaned, hand batting the side table until she found her ringing phone. Her "hello" was muffled.

"Leah," Tasha's bubbly voice came through clearly on the other end. "I'm so glad I caught you. I hope I didn't wake you."

Leah cleared her throat and rubbed her eyes, trying to force herself back into the land of the conscious. She and Liam had…reunited in every room of the house the day before.

"No worries, I was just getting up. What's going on?"

Liam laughed softly beside her at the obvious lie. She bit her lip at the sight of him, the sheet slung low on his hip, baring a deliciously distracting stretch of skin.

Tasha's voice on the other end of the line eventually broke through the cloud of lust. Shaking her head, she got up, abandoning the vision in her bed to concentrate on her other dream come true. "I'm sorry, Tash, what was that?"

Tasha laughed on the other end of the line. "I said, 'Darling, if you aren't feeling awake yet, be prepared.'"

"You've got my attention."

"Mr. Alderson reached out to me. He mentioned speaking with you at your shrimp boil slash play slash investors' meeting. I'll forgive you for not extending the invitation, but only because you knew I had a big show going on at the time. In the future, I expect an invitation regardless."

Leah laughed softly. She loved this woman. "You got it: no more withheld invitations."

"Good, glad we're on the same page now. I know you chatted with him at the gallery; did he mention reaching out to me?"

"He did, yeah. He mentioned being cautious about intermingling the two projects too much. He's interested in investing in a potential venture here at the farm."

Leah waited for Tasha's noise of affirmation before continuing, "Anyway, it was amazing spinning out some thoughts with him and a local couple. Trying to figure out the best way forward kept me up all night."

"Oh, I can imagine."

Leah laughed. "Woe is me, the answer to my dreams falling into my lap."

Tasha laughed. "No, girl. I do actually understand that. When the gallery was finally coming together, and then again when it started turning an actual livable profit, I freaked out. Anything I can weigh in on?"

"He mentioned being interested in pursuing some commission pieces and also working together on the farm. I assume there's an end to his line of capital, so I need to send some numbers to him. I really want to work with him on the art. There's so much I'd like to explore with the dragon theme, but I really need this farm to work. I'm just not sure if he realized the capital needed when we spoke last night, and I really don't want to choose." She sighed. "That's greedy, I know."

Tasha's laughter on the other end of the line sent a stab of hurt through her.

Tasha wheezed out a final laugh. "Sorry, sorry. It's just... Before you get mad at me, let me explain. Maybe I can shed some light. He will definitely need some details from you about the level of funding that would be appropriate. If you're the project manager on the farm thing, you're not going to have much time to pursue the art without burning yourself out. If you hire someone to assist with the farm, you can do both. Based on my conversation with him, that's his main concern."

"Oh," Leah said, voice faint. "I don't think I can afford to hire someone to assist with this."

Tasha laughed again on the other end of the line. "Girl, he's super rich. Not super great with the communication of all of his grand ideas, which is why he likes to have a go-between who knows him better. He would be willing *and able* to front the salary of someone to assist with the farm project. It would put the venture a little more in his pocket, which he knows some people are a little leery of. But, it would also give you time to focus on the dream you've been dreaming."

Leah blinked, hope fluttering in her chest. "I did not know that," she said slowly.

"He doesn't love to flaunt it. Too many people trying to take advantage and the like. Anyway, back to the reason he reached out to me to be the go between on the art. And then you and I can discuss, or you can discuss with someone else, on the next steps. He's interested in setting you up with a large commission. A series of interconnected pieces. He adored what you did with the dragon, and he'd love to see something with a central piece and several smaller related pieces."

"Okay, wow. How large are we talking?"

When Tasha told her, Leah sat down hard on one of the kitchen chairs. Between the likely advance on that, the money she'd pulled together thus far, and pulling from her retirement, she could refinance the mortgage with

Paige's bank. She could swing the mortgage without even doing anything with the farm.

"Still there, dear?"

Leah cleared her throat. "Yeah, sorry, I'm here."

"You sitting down?"

"You could've asked that earlier."

Tasha laughed brightly. "Any questions? Want to go back to discussing the other pet project he'd like to pursue with you?"

Leah's mind whirred. "I don't suppose you happen to know the advance on that commission, do you?"

"I'm glad to hear you're interested. We should meet, hammer out some of his expectations before you commit to anything. And there's one more thing you should know before you finalize lining up the metaphorical ducks of your future plans."

Leah grinned. Whatever Tasha had to say, she was elated.

"Your pieces sold, Leah," Tasha said warmly. "Congratulations."

Leah squealed, holding the phone away from her in deference to not bursting Tasha's eardrums. Officially a professional fucking artist over here. "How many?" she asked, biting her lip.

She caught sight of Liam leaning in the doorway of the bedroom. She grinned at him and wiggled out a happy dance in her chair, delighting in his familiar grin and dancing eyes.

She *almost* missed Tasha's answer through her elation. "I'm going to need you to say that again."

"All of them."

"Holy shit, holy shit, holy shit."

"Don't hyperventilate, dear. Go celebrate. You've earned it. I've already sent the funds for direct deposit. Should be in your account and available in the next few days for whatever hanky panky you'd like to get up to."

"Thank you, thank you, thank you. Oh my God, Tasha, thank you!"

Tasha laughed. "You're welcome, chica. Now, go. We can discuss the rest later."

She launched herself into Liam's arms, diving straight into a mind-melting kiss. When they separated, he grinned boyishly before gathering her more securely into his arms and spinning her around the kitchen.

When he set her down, he cupped her face in his hands as she beamed at him, dizzy with elation. Or possibly the spinning. Probably it was both. Both was good.

"Good news, then?"

She gave him a dopey grin. "The best."

His eyes twinkled with happiness, and she felt the last piece click into place. Miles away from the plan and all the better for it.

Author's Note

Any negative impressions of Leah's law firm are *not* inspired by my own experiences at the firm where I worked. I was fortunate to work with an excellent crew of people, and my life is brighter for having known and worked with them. (Thank you to my law firm family!) Unlike Leah, my own exit was heralded by health issues. Like Leah, I had many frustrations with practicing family law (as do so many working in this area). I am beyond grateful for the people at my firm and in the legal community who made the practice easier. A more particular thank you to the ladies of my firm. You all are absolutely amazing, phenomenally competent, and I am so delighted to have had the opportunity to work with you.

Writing this book was a delightful, crazy, *trying* ride. I started this novel at the end of 2021. Days before I promised myself I'd start writing it, I lost a loved one. On top of the other life events I was dealing with at the time, it was almost enough to see this project derailed. Instead, I took some of the emotions I was feeling and dumped them onto Leah. Some of those spiraling down scenes were removed in the interests of keeping the book moving forward but writing them was well worth it. At the end here, I have also noticed that several of the mentions of Grayson were also cut, but I assure you, he's there, keeping an eye out.

Health issues and various other life events pushed this book to the back burner until I made my own (teary) exit from my law firm. (Shout out to the law firm bestie who heard me gushing about these characters and then watched in frustration as I set them aside. Thank you for the amazing conversations and being who you are.)

For something I was thinking about and working on for months upon months, it's absolutely surreal that it's here. I'm going to be holding this in my hands! And oh my gosh, to the people who have taken the time to read the book, *thank you*.

Acknowledgements

All of the gratitude to the main Cassidy/Madison in my life for *all the things* (in particular, the emotional roller coaster ride I took you on). Pieces of you are in both characters, so it's unsurprising they're two of my favorites. Also, for not only letting me gush about my love for my characters but for actually enjoying the gushing, *thank you*.

To my parents, thank you also for all of the things. Thank you for encouraging in me a love of reading, and thank you for the foundation you helped me build for the rest of my life. For everything you gave me and taught me: Thank you times one-thousand.

In writing this section, I realize I have *so many* people who deserve a thank you for the support and the encouragement to live my best life. I'm trying to be a little anonymous here, so you'll be unnamed. (Also turns out there are a lot of you!)

Thank you to the people who were so immediately excited at the idea of this book. There were not a lot of you due in large part to my superstition it simply wouldn't happen, if I told too many people. So, *thank you*. Your excitement was fuel when this project became *work*.

Becky, I'm sorry you didn't make it into the book! I hope this acknowledgment can tide you over. ;-)

Finally, thank you to Mountains Wanted Publishing for the line edits and to MIBLART for the gorgeous cover!

Made in the USA
Monee, IL
29 December 2023

50771923R00129